FUJINO OMORI

ILLUSTRATION BY
KIYOTAKA HAIMURA

CHARACTER DESIGN BY
SUZUHITO YASUDA

*"I...want
to become
stronger."*

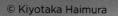

Is it WRONG
to TRY to
PICK UP GIRLS
in a DUNGEON?
ON THE
SIDE

*Sword
Oratoria*

CONTENTS

PROLOGUE ♦ A Torturous Night, a Ghastly Gloom 001

CHAPTER 1 ♦ Why I'll Start Running, Too 005

CHAPTER 2 ♦ The Decisive Battle Intermission 029

CHAPTER 3 ♦ The True Face of a God 053

CHAPTER 4 ♦ Avengers ~Knossos War~ 081

CHAPTER 5 ♦ Obsession Manifest 119

CHAPTER 6 ♦ And Then the God Smiled 148

EPILOGUE ♦ Whodunit 196

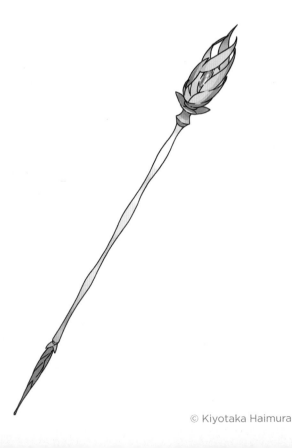

© Kiyotaka Haimura

"But I'm going to go out on a limb and ask: Let us participate in your plan...

s are yed,

e...

you."

DIONYSUS:
Patron god of *Dionysus Familia*.
Looking to avenge his followers.

Before Knossos's entrance, the familia members standing around the prum holding his long spear adopted tense looks and readied themselves for battle.

"If we're going all out, how about a visit to my home village? Before long, the Great Tree will have its crown of light."

...Until all mastermind uncovered and destro I won't be able to complete my objectiv Please, Loki. I beg of

"Once this is all done, we'll go. **I promise.**"

FILVIS CHALLIA:
Captain of *Dionysus Familia*.
A magic swordswoman.

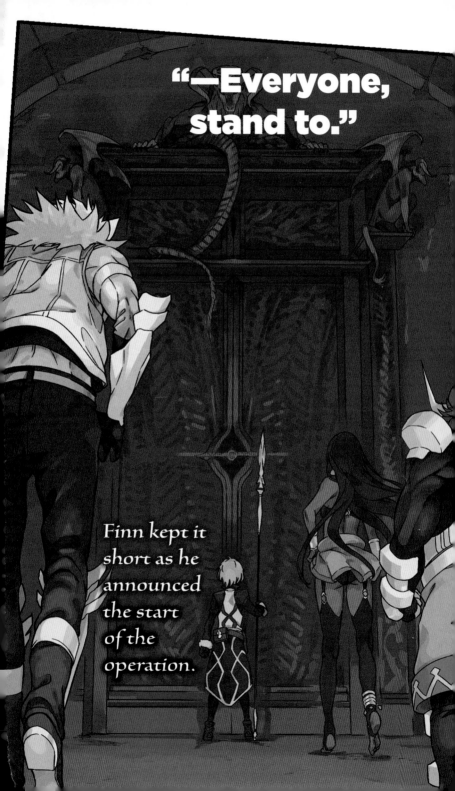

"—Everyone, stand to."

Finn kept it short as he announced the start of the operation.

VOLUME 11

FUJINO OMORI

ILLUSTRATION BY
KIYOTAKA HAIMURA

CHARACTER DESIGN BY
SUZUHITO YASUDA

NEW YORK

IS IT WRONG TO TRY TO PICK UP GIRLS IN A DUNGEON?
ON THE SIDE: SWORD ORATORIA, Volume 11
FUJINO OMORI

Translation by Dale DeLucia
Cover art by Kiyotaka Haimura

This book is a work of fiction. Names, characters, places, and incidents are the product of the author's imagination or are used fictitiously. Any resemblance to actual events, locales, or persons, living or dead, is coincidental.

DUNGEON NI DEAI WO MOTOMERU NO WA MACHIGATTEIRUDAROUKA GAIDEN
SWORD ORATORIA vol. 11
Copyright © 2019 Fujino Omori
Illustration copyright © 2019 Kiyotaka Haimura
Original Character Design © Suzuhito Yasuda
All rights reserved.
Original Japanese edition published in 2019 by SB Creative Corp.
This English edition is published by arrangement with SB Creative Corp., Tokyo, in care of Tuttle-Mori Agency, Inc., Tokyo.

English translation © 2020 by Yen Press, LLC

Yen Press, LLC supports the right to free expression and the value of copyright. The purpose of copyright is to encourage writers and artists to produce the creative works that enrich our culture.

The scanning, uploading, and distribution of this book without permission is a theft of the author's intellectual property. If you would like permission to use material from the book (other than for review purposes), please contact the publisher. Thank you for your support of the author's rights.

Yen On
150 West 30th Street, 19th Floor
New York, NY 10001

Visit us at yenpress.com
facebook.com/yenpress
twitter.com/yenpress
yenpress.tumblr.com
instagram.com/yenpress

First Yen On Edition: February 2020

Yen On is an imprint of Yen Press, LLC.
The Yen On name and logo are trademarks of Yen Press, LLC.

The publisher is not responsible for websites (or their content) that are not owned by the publisher.

Library of Congress Cataloging-in-Publication Data
Names: Ōmori, Fujino, author. | Haimura, Kiyotaka, 1973– illustrator. | Yasuda, Suzuhito, designer.
Title: Is it wrong to try to pick up girls in a dungeon? on the side: sword oratoria / story by Fujino Omori; illustration by Kiyotaka Haimura; original design by Suzuhito Yasuda.
Other titles: Danjon ni deai wo motomeru no wa machigatteirudarouka gaiden sword oratoria. English.
Description: New York, NY: Yen On, 2016– | Series: Is it wrong to try to pick up girls in a dungeon? on the side: sword oratoria
Identifiers: LCCN 2016023729 | ISBN 9780316315333 (v. 1 : pbk.) | ISBN 9780316318167 (v. 2 : pbk.) | ISBN 9780316318181 (v. 3 : pbk.) | ISBN 9780316318228 (v. 4 : pbk.) | ISBN 9780316442503 (v. 5 : pbk.) | ISBN 9780316442527 (v. 6 : pbk.) | ISBN 9781975302863 (v. 7 : pbk.) | ISBN 9781975327798 (v. 8 : pbk.) | ISBN 9781975327811 (v. 9 : pbk.) | ISBN 9781975331719 (v. 10 : pbk.) | ISBN 9781975331733 (v. 11 : pbk.)
Subjects: CYAC: Fantasy.
Classification: LCC PZ7.1.O54 Isg 2016 | DDC [Fic]—dc23
LC record available at https://lccn.loc.gov/2016023729

ISBNs: 978-1-9753-3173-3 (paperback)
978-1-9753-3174-0 (ebook)

1 3 5 7 9 10 8 6 4 2

LSC-C

Printed in the United States of America

VOLUME 11

FUJINO OMORI

ILLUSTRATION BY **KIYOTAKA HAIMURA**
CHARACTER DESIGN BY **SUZUHITO YASUDA**

A TORTUROUS NIGHT, A GHASTLY GLOOM

Гэта казка іншага сям'і.

Ноч пакут, якая ўзвышаецца цемра

The battle cry of a young man melded together with a minotaur's ferocious roar. A vicious fight was raging.

With their lives on the line, the two males threw themselves into mortal combat, both launching starry sparks into the air as they tried to drive home with Labrys ax or knife. The throngs of people enclosing their battleground prayed, crying out with enough force to make the city quake.

Praying for the victory of the boy who'd set off on his adventure.

Praying for the birth of a new hero.

Aiz silently observed this violent scene unfolding in the Labyrinth City.

"………"

The werewolf by her side, along with an elf and a dark-elf swordsman—all counted among the ranks of first-tier adventurers—could not pull their eyes away from that battle.

Five months prior, a similar fight against a minotaur in the Dungeon had fascinated the adventurers of *Loki Familia*. The battle, howl, and will of this young boy were bound to light a fire in the hearts of many—the entire city, even.

But Aiz's heart wasn't pounding in her chest the way it had the time before.

Trapped in the dark, she felt closed off from the frenzied world—as if she'd stumbled into a maze with no exit, as if she were a child who had nowhere left to return.

The only image that reached her eyes seemed to be that of the young boy who bled, cloaked in flames.

She kept thinking, wondering what was on his mind as he fought.

His answer had contradicted hers. For what reason was he battling a monster and to what end? There was little doubt that this was a fight to the death, but it appeared as though the boy and the minotaur yearned for this from each other, like they understood each other more than anyone else—leaving Aiz behind.

Try as she might, Aiz couldn't come up with a convincing conclusion.

But she did understand one thing.

He would become stronger.

He would start running again.

He would overcome this trial—a night filled with heretical monsters. This would become the day that the boy who had become an adventurer a scant five months ago would set off on the path to becoming a hero.

—And what about me as I am now?

Uncertainty had begun to fester on Aiz's sword.

Her vow to kill monsters had been broken.

When she'd challenged that boy's will with her own, she'd been the one who'd lost.

—Can I become strong like him?

—Can I start running, too?

At the moment, his gallant figure and her current state could not possibly be any more different. The fleeting thoughts that she'd managed to cling to soon faded away.

And even though she'd asked and asked, the stars and moon winking in the night sky offered no answer.

Darkness settled in, impenetrable and dismal. A stagnant chill. An ear-ringing solitude. The murky gloom was writhing like a living creature, the ultimate embodiment of chaos.

In an unknown place—in reality, or illusion, or somewhere in between—a shadow stood erect, waiting impatiently, counting down to a moment that would soon arrive.

"*—Enyo.*"

A blinding ray of light revealed the silhouette of the one who had called out, whose race and gender were unknown, their identity concealed by a masked face. The figure spoke in an ominous voice that mixed together an array of overlapping human voices.

"Loki Familia *is...coming to Knossos.*"

Upon hearing that report, the named shadow's lips curled into a sneer, announcing that the finale was drawing near.

It was an expression that seemed almost cheerful, almost reluctant, almost rapturous, almost lonely—and almost trembling.

The shadow turned their back to the masked being, who stood in silence, and raised both hands like a conductor preparing to begin.

—To begin a beautiful *orgia.*

WHY I'LL START RUNNING, TOO

Гэта казка іншага сям і.

Так я і пачаць працаваць

"We made a deal with the armed monsters."

Let me start with the final decision. After Finn led with that prefacing remark, the room fell into hushed silence for a moment before breaking into an uproar.

They were in the large dining room of *Loki Familia*'s home, Twilight Manor.

Almost every single one of the faction's members had been summoned, filling the seats and lining the walls. There was no way anyone could have expected a different reaction to their captain's proclamation or that there wouldn't at least be a handful who struggled to comprehend, left reeling from the shock.

The emblem of the trickster with its ridiculous grin hung behind Finn, who stood atop a seat at the head of the table in the back of the hall. Standing at his sides were Riveria, Gareth, and their patron goddess, Loki. The presence of these three was confirmation that Finn hadn't made this arbitrary decision alone and was instead a point of consensus among the familia's leadership. It wasn't just Raul, Anakity, and other elite candidates who were wide-eyed. Tiona and Tione weren't much more composed than their juniors.

The only ones who weren't flustered were Lefiya and the others in the Fairy Force, who had participated in the assault on Knossos—and, surprisingly, Bete.

"What are you talking about, Captain?!"

"What do you mean, 'made a deal'?!"

The members of the familia leaped to their feet, shoving chairs out of the way and shouting in bewilderment, confusion, and even something close to blame.

It was an unbelievable scene for *Loki Familia*, a tight-knit group brought together by their leader, Braver. It was out of place to see them up in arms against Finn and spoke to the magnitude of the problem that his proposal would create.

The younger girls jolted and cowed under thundering protests and threatening behavior, but Finn did not waver in the slightest, facing the storm of shouts and responding to every question.

"During the battle in Daedalus Street, I confirmed the armed monsters have extremely high intelligence—to the point that there appeared to be a chance of coming to a mutual understanding with them."

"'Mutual understanding'...You're telling me you let that stop you?!"

"Of course not. I just saw that they possessed a certain intelligence in their eyes that was worth considering. I judged that sufficient grounds to make a deal with them."

"And where's the proof that those monsters won't turn on us?!"

"There's no way to prove their emotions—even for the gods... That said, it's a hard fact that the number of resident and adventurer casualties resulting from this incident with the monsters was zero."

"...Gh!"

"Sure, we can say it was because every adventurer in the city gave their all, but that wouldn't explain how we managed to avoid even a single loss of life despite the catastrophic turn of events...It'd be out of character for the monsters we're familiar with. Allow me to make that objective observation."

Finn didn't beat around the bush in laying out his reasoning. He knew that would have the opposite effect, which was why he frankly answered all the questions lobbed at him.

He let them vent their hesitation, dissatisfaction, rage, hatred— explaining everything in his own words without making any attempt to quibble with their arguments. He would never try to force his view on them with rhetorical flourishes. Without raising his voice, he appealed to them with the available information, responding with a dispassionate tone that carried across the room.

At this moment, Finn wasn't engaging in a discussion but a

ritual—not offering an explanation so much as getting them to sympathize with his cause, all in order to move forward.

"I've already completed negotiations with a group of armed monsters during the battle two days ago. Bearing witness to this are none other than Lefiya and her companions who stormed Knossos with her."

"What...?!"

"This might have been something that I should have kept from you...If I'm being frank, I'd intended to hide it, even though I knew about the true nature of those monsters—all because I predicted that the familia would be thrown into disarray, like it is now," Finn revealed, sincere, earnest, resolute.

Without any deceit, Finn gave them a glimpse of his thoughts and hopes, and the barrage of voices assaulting him died off for a beat.

"...Then why...why are you bringing it up?" a male familia member finally ventured.

"To win," Finn declared to his confused subordinate, who looked as if he was begging for some sort of explanation. "To defeat those denizens of darkness who are lurking inside that lair of demons. To ensure peace for Orario. For that, I would even become a villain," he finished with unwavering resolve.

He announced his willingness to throw away the fame he had clung onto so tightly, to become an enemy to humanity if that's what it took.

Just like Bell Cranell had—and Finn knew that an even more tragic end would await him for it.

In truth, he had not given up on the path of the hero in the slightest. Just as he had told Riveria and Gareth, he had sworn to himself that he would return an even greater one if he fell into notoriety.

But to those familia members who had no way of knowing about his growth, which had happened behind the scenes, this came as an unimaginable shock. No, even if they had known, it would have only made the impact all the bigger. They were at a loss for words because they knew just how much Finn had devoted himself to the restoration of his race.

His determination toward this cause shook them to their very cores.

"Any more comments? I'll answer anything. I intend to give it to you straight in response to your concerns and thoughts."

The protests had come to an end after their prum leader answered every comment, systematic and unflinching, during the drawn-out assembly. By this point, even members who had been the most vocal about their disapproval had uneasily pursed their lips. The others exchanged glances, unsure of what to say.

But there were those who stayed silent for other reasons: There was no way they could beat Finn in an argument. They were the members of *Loki Familia* who hadn't been able to dispel their hatred of monsters. For those with unresolved issues from losing a loved one to a monster, this animosity ran deep, unbridgeable no matter how forthright Finn was in his answers.

If anyone had dashed out of the room then, all of those who had been alienated by his proposal would surely follow in a chain reaction.

That was when Anakity raised her slender arm straight into the air, as if cutting through the noise. "Captain."

"Yes, Aki?"

"No posturing or lip service. Can you tell us what *you* think of the armed monsters?" The cat person slowly stood up from her chair, speaking as though she was testing him.

Finn responded in a tone no different from all his other responses. "I'd like to say that we can use them…but I'm going to make it a point to say…I trust them. I believe those monsters are worthy of it."

Trust. The familia members were troubled by this word.

Maintaining the same expression, Anakity came back with a follow-up question. "There are those among us who have had friends, family, lovers slaughtered by monsters. Are you still saying that you trust them?"

"I am."

Say there were dwarves whose comrades had been killed by elves or elves whose brethren had been murdered by dwarves. Would they bear a grudge against the perpetrator's entire race?

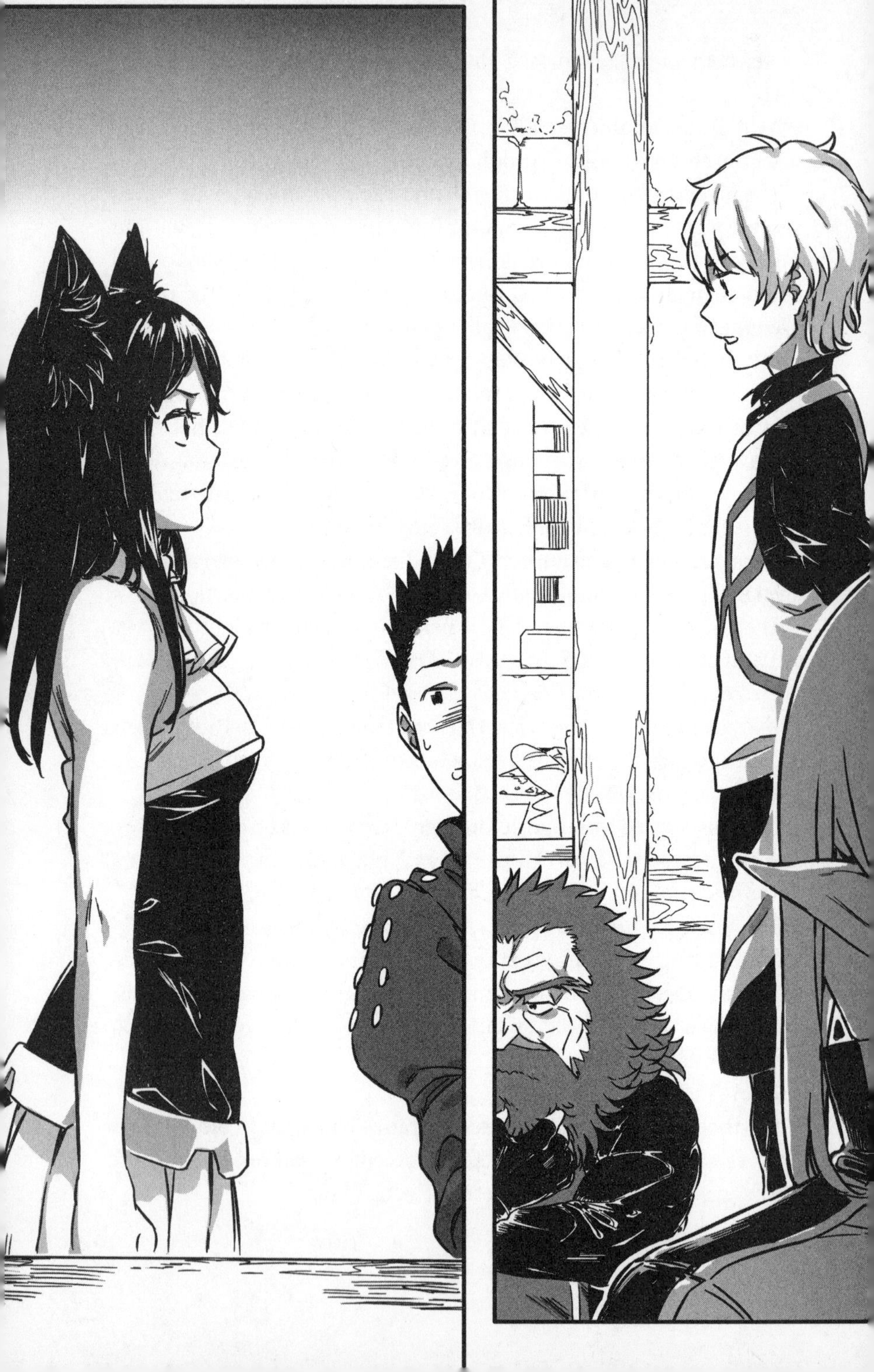

—Not that Finn would respond with this cliché.

He knew monsters were humanity's enemy, a malignant tumor on the mortal realm that needed to be removed at all costs. And yet, he declared that he would take a swig of their poison.

No petty tricks. He'd chosen to show his determination with one simple idea instead of a roundabout explanation.

Because if he couldn't even do that, how could they possibly hope to fight side by side with the monsters?

Anakity stared into Finn's blue eyes, which concealed nothing, and bore his decision.

"…"

Her eyes, as black as her hair, were probing him. It was the gaze of someone appraising another who held the higher Status. Not that it was impolite. It was well within the rights granted to a lower-tier member in an organization. Without it, an organization would reject a great many ideas and stunt its growth.

Anakity Autumn looked at him for the others in the room—the eyes of the people. In effect, she spoke for everyone else.

The one who couldn't break into the big leagues, Raul, flicked his gaze back and forth between the girl in his cohort and his beloved captain. His distress was almost charming.

"…Okay. Then I have nothing else to say." Anakity silently sat back down.

It signaled that she would follow Finn's resolution, which pacified the other familia members for the simple reason that Anakity had agreed to it.

This change of heart wasn't something that the leaders or top-tier adventurers, including Finn and Aiz, would have been able to achieve. It had to be done by Anakity, who headed the second-string forces that connected all lower-tier members to the elites.

Winning over Aki is big…Well, I guess she skillfully directed it, huh?

He wouldn't let anyone know he sincerely thought from the bottom of his heart that she'd just saved him. If he'd been anything less than completely committed, Anakity would have cast him aside for the sake of the other familia members. With her gifts and impartiality, she could carry it out—easy.

Though she'd respected and sworn loyalty to the familia's leaders, she had a strong enough will to defy them if their actions were illogical. But she was wise. She understood what the familia needed as they prepared to conduct an attack on Knossos—namely, solidarity.

She had posed her question to test Finn—and to understand his intentions. It could even be said that she did so because she trusted him. It was clear that her shrewdness had brought the familia closer together.

"May I…say something?"

The last to raise her hand was the elf Alicia. When Finn nodded, she stood up, placing her hand on her chest.

"One of those armed monsters…saved my life," she confessed, as if in repentance, causing a stir to spread through the room.

Her face was awash with a complicated expression, anguished, as though she had not yet come to a decision herself. The Fairy Force, including Lefiya, who had seen the event from start to finish, looked on supportively.

"It wasn't some coincidence—or a whim. That siren covered me of her own volition. Even at the cost of her own body…she protected me with a spirit that can only be called philia—friendship. I'm still haunted by her gaze and smile…"

Though Alicia had a gentle side as an elder of the group, everyone knew that beyond it was her elven pride and fastidiousness. And if she was feeling something other than scorn toward a monster, no one in *Loki Familia* was stupid enough to fail to understand what that meant.

"I don't want to admit or accept it. But I can't help thinking…that was a noble display of her selflessness. If I failed to admit that, I feared I would become lower than the monsters—a dishonorable beast," Alicia finished, carefully choosing her words and choking them out.

The moment she slipped back into her chair, drained, the room fell totally silent. Even all the other outspoken elves closed their mouths.

"...I've changed the order around, but I'd like to go back to the premise that led me to this conclusion."

In the quiet room, Finn began to explain the current situation.

"In order to differentiate them from other monsters, I'm going to refer to the armed monsters as Xenos from now on. Because of their high levels of intelligence and apparent self-awareness, the Xenos have had countless of their comrades hunted by *Ikelos Familia*."

"!"

"As far as the Xenos are concerned, the forces inside Knossos related to the smuggling of monsters are their enemies. I won't go so far as to say that an enemy of an enemy is an ally, but...our interests are undeniably aligned. And just this one time, we can direct them as needed. That was my conclusion."

"But, Captain, that means..."

"That's right. We made a deal to temporarily join forces this one time. It's for the sake of taking on Knossos...for the sake of ensuring victory in the coming battle, where the fate of the city hangs in the balance."

By this point, Finn was simply discussing justifications for their actions while arguing in his sagacious and sound way.

It provided just cause for suddenly dropping such volatile news, softening the blow by shuffling the order of his delivery to manage their expectations. And Finn's plan had clearly worked, given how even the members who had gnashed their teeth at the news were noticeably less tense.

Starting with why the Xenos had come aboveground, Finn continued to divulge all relevant information. Of course, he hid the connection between Ouranos and the Xenos to prevent further disorder, but other than that, he shared everything.

Gareth and Riveria spoke for the first time to bolster his explanation.

"We're not saying you have to meet halfway with all monsters. The opposite, in fact. I'd actually say you shouldn't trust them at all."

"When you explore the Dungeon in the future, keep in mind that hesitation will get you killed. I understand it is asking a lot of you, but detach your identity as adventurers from this situation."

Gareth had aimed his address at primarily the men. And looks of understanding spread among the elves at Riveria's statement.

Finally, as if measuring her timing, Loki announced her divine will. "Well, basically, this is a battle to avenge Leene and the rest, so we'll use whatever we hafta."

A short speech, but the results were immediate. At the very least, there was no one left who would openly voice their opposition.

"...Let's end this here. I'd like you all to take a moment to think and talk among yourselves. Okay? This isn't an order but a suggestion. I'd like you to mull it over."

Finn looked out at the faces of all the familia members again, saving the golden eyes of a certain girl for last.

"If anyone wishes to abstain, come to my office. I have no intention of trying to stop you. I'll ask you to keep our discussion secret but nothing more. I'll respect your decision. Okay, then—you're all dismissed."

With that, Finn left the room with Loki and the other leaders.

Once they took their leave, a furious exchange of opinions ensued among almost all the familia members who'd stayed behind in the dining hall. There was no end of things to discuss, and those who had felt suffocated by the atmosphere before could finally speak their minds.

Hesitation. Bewilderment. Rage. Hatred. Fear. None of these emotions were inherently wrong, but none were entirely right, either. They continued engaging in heated discussions about the relations between people and monsters—starting from when they were summoned in the morning until being dismissed at noon. The sky gradually darkened, bringing out the stars, as the conversations carried into the evening.

"It's the first time I've seen the familia act like this...I think you all might be glaring more than when we went on the expedition... Urgh..."

Raul wobbled like a ghost before almost collapsing into a chair. He sat down at the table with Anakity and the rest of the reserve members, plus Tiona and Tione.

With raised voices, the lower-tier adventurers had roasted Raul, scapegoating him with their discontent and grumbling. Unlike Bete, he could be dragged into conversations and become the target of their complaints, which was why he had their trust (?). He had done his best to seriously and kindly listen to everyone, even though that ended up totally exhausting him. He sprawled out on the table, facedown, as Anakity patted the back of his head.

There was no change in her expression, but it seemed like she was showing her appreciation to him for serving this critical role or perhaps she was simply saying he had done a good job.

"By the way…what do you all think?"

"…I guess I'm fine either way. As long as we can get our revenge on the guys who killed Leene, Lloyd, and the others. That said, I've got some reservations about borrowing the strength of a monster…"

Raul had peeled himself off the table as he asked his question. Around him, Lefiya, Rakuta, and other female familia members were bustling about to distribute sandwiches, unable to sit still while everyone else kept arguing without even having lunch.

The one to respond to his timid question was the chienthrope Cruz, a Level-4 member of the junior members like Raul, who crossed his arms.

"But…but, Cruuuuz! They're monsters! Aren't you scared?" Lefiya's roommate, Elfie, cut in.

"Well, yeah, it's scary. We'll be fighting with them, after all…If that black minotaur comes out…yeah, I'd jump out of my skin! I'm definitely uneasy about it!" The Level-4 human Narfi chimed in, shivering as she held herself, seemingly remembering the sensation of that bloodcurdling howl on Daedalus Street.

"B-but it's the captain. He must have a plan…Erm, though it'd be impossible to work together…But I guess all we can do is trust him. This isn't really the time to be fighting among ourselves…"

All Raul could utter was a noncommittal opinion.

"Are you dumbasses still at it?"

"B-Bete…"

His ashen hair billowing, the werewolf barged in and cut through the dining hall to get something to eat. He was one of the few people who had left promptly upon dismissal, ignoring those who had stayed behind arguing. Bete was maintaining his lone-wolf act, but for once, he didn't try to make fun of the people discussing the armed monsters. Settling at a spot one table away from Raul, he scraped the chair across the floor before hunkering down.

When he turned his gaze to Rakuta, the hume bunny girl scurried back to the kitchen to fix him whatever supper was left.

"…Hey, Bete. What do you think of the armed monsters?"

"What?"

Tiona had been quiet all this time and used this opportunity to speak up, which the werewolf must not have expected. His voice sounded weird, and he looked uncharacteristically startled.

"…Have *you* made up your mind?"

"Erm…Well, I didn't realize everyone was gonna be so worried and upset about the whole thing, so I actually tried my hardest to rack my brain, but…" admitted one of the Amazonian twins, who was generally considered a bad thinker by everyone—including herself. Sitting cross-legged in her chair, she folded her arms, groaning in thought, as she closed her eyes and nodded to herself.

But it didn't seem that her answer was going to change, because she opened her eyes and said, "I don't think we need to be afraid of those monsters."

"!"

"Finn said it, too: Those armed monsters haven't hurt anyone. And I saw one of them protect a kid on the street."

Tiona didn't mention that the one she had spotted was the vouivre, but she did tell them about everything else. Raul and the others were thunderstruck. As with Alicia's tale, hearing about a monster protecting a person was mind-bending—a contradiction to an inherent truth of the world.

Everyone around them naturally listened in on the conversation among elites.

"At least I thought it wouldn't be so bad to fight together with those armed monsters...Um, Xenos, was it?" Tiona laughed thoughtlessly.

As Narfi and the others felt unsettled by her sloppy grin, Bete shot her an exasperated look and glanced over at Tione.

She had stayed behind in the dining hall due to her younger sister's insistent badgering, even though she was fed up with everything. When she noticed his gaze, she audibly snorted.

"That's what the captain decided! I'm gonna follow his lead, even if it means fighting alongside the filthy monsters!"

"You're damn consistent, ya know that...?" Bete was so beyond dumbfounded that he even felt a little respect for her undying belief in her beloved captain.

Raul and the others shared a wry smile.

"And what about you? What side are you on? I figured you would have blown up right away," Tiona retorted.

"It ain't a joke if the city goes under because we're cooped up here complaining. That's all," Bete responded, sounding almost bored.

"..."

"At the end of the day, I can air my grievances and bloodlust all I want in the Dungeon. Gramps and the old hag said it, too. We're adventurers. That doesn't change. Am I wrong?"

Bete's response was simple, though he was choosing his words carefully. His amber eyes flashed, as though he was remembering something he'd seen two days earlier during the battle on Daedalus Street. In fact, his explanation was so straightforward that it didn't allow any room for debate, silencing the familia members who were listening.

"Assholes who just want to complain can go ahead and leave the familia. That's all there is to it."

"Oooh, someone thinks he's cool. You're such a poseur."

"You're the one who asked me, you dumb Amazon!"

Watching Raul and the others lunging to stop the first-tier adventurers from fighting—an everyday scene in *Loki Familia*—everyone who had been furrowing their brows all day started to break into smiles here and there.

After tussling with Bete for a while, Tiona whirled around with disheveled hair, turning her attention on a certain girl. "What do you think, Lefiya?"

"I..."

After distributing refreshments, Lefiya had been watching their exchange from a few steps away. She finally shared her thoughts in her honest way. "I'm afraid of the monsters...but I get the feeling those ones might be different."

"Different?"

"Unlike every other monster we've come across in the Dungeon... they didn't evoke the same sort of intrinsic hatred."

She was thinking, of course, about the siren who had protected Alicia. The scene that she'd witnessed during the retreat from the battle with the Evils' Remnants was stuck in the back of her mind. She was afraid that her next comment might cause her friends to shun or criticize her, but she pushed forward, clearly articulating her thoughts.

"I think...those monsters have hearts that care about their comrades...like elves and everyone else."

Lefiya's voice echoed through the dining hall. There was a brief moment of silence before Tiona broke into a smile and pounced on her with a big hug.

"Yeah! Yeah! Me too! Those monsters care about their friends!"

"M-Miss Tiona...!"

The monsters cared about their friends. It may have been the strangest thing that could be said, but there was certainly enough evidence to come to that conclusion. The other familia members had fallen into silent reflection, as if preoccupied with their recollections of the battle that had raged in the Labyrinth District. Bete scoffed and Tione sighed, while Raul and the others wore strained smiles, but there was no doubt that Tiona's innocent outburst had shattered the tension and helped everyone relax.

Even Lefiya caught her infectious laugh, finding a little peace of mind.

"..."

But her face clouded over as her gaze landed on an empty seat. It was where the girl with golden hair and eyes had sat, the first to leave the dining hall after Finn's talk was over.

Moonlight streamed in through the window. Beyond it spanned the navy sky, dressing the unlit room in a dark purple.

The noise coming from the great hall was distant, muffled. In fact, her room was so quiet, it was hard to believe both spaces were part of the same manor. It was as though it had fallen off the edge of the world.

"..."

Wearing a plain white dress, Aiz wasn't doing anything in particular as she sat on top of her bed, hugging her knees to her chest. She buried her face gently between them, her long eyelashes trembling as she looked down at the sheets. The moonlight rested on her slender ankles.

"Aiz, I'm coming in."

There was a gentle knock on the wooden door that echoed through the room.

Paying no heed to the lack of response, Riveria entered. As she came to a halt with the closed door behind her, she looked at Aiz sitting atop her bed, deep in thought. Riveria fell silent.

For the past two days, *Loki Familia* had been swamped dealing with the cleanup from the Xenos emerging aboveground. The bulk of it had been repairing and cleaning up Daedalus Street, which had become a battlefield, where a rapid rebuild of the district was underway. *Loki Familia* was proactively taking part in that day in and day out. They had no choice in the matter, really.

On top of that, thanks to Ouranos's maneuverings, the Guild had publicly declared that *Loki Familia* had eliminated all the armed monsters, which meant Finn, Riveria, and Gareth had to deal with that as the ones in charge. And in Riveria's case, she had to take care of Alicia and the other elves who had interacted directly with the

Xenos. It had been an extremely busy few days, during which she had not had any time to talk to the girl before her, even though it had been clear she was in a terrible state.

"…Aiz. What happened on that day?"

Aiz had hardly opened her mouth at all since then. She had not tried to interact with anyone and responded with only the bare minimum when Lefiya or Tiona or the others tried to engage her. She was trapped inside a prison of anguish. Riveria had come to understand this.

"…" Aiz did not answer the question posed to her by the high elf graced with fluttering jade hair. Instead, she responded with one of her own: "Riveria…do heroes exist?"

That was her question. Aiz herself did not understand why she'd asked it.

"Are there heroes for certain people…for one person? Do they exist?"

"…"

They were pointless questions. Ones without answers. What flashed through Aiz's mind was the boy who stood against her in order to protect a monster girl—and the tears of a dragon girl, onto which she had projected her younger self. These scenes from two days ago were still haunting her.

"…Those who wait for a hero end up dying in obscurity. Or at least, that's how the majority of them meet their ends. Only a handful are ever found by one."

Aiz seemed lost, but there was almost a sense of pleading in her words. In response, Riveria gave the logical answer. It was a self-evident truth. Aiz lowered her eyes, hiding her doll-like features, as she started to talk in fragments.

"I couldn't cut it down…A monster."

"…"

"Not because it could speak. Not because it seemed human…but because it cried."

"…"

"The way I did back then…"

"…"

"And I thought…Bell and that vouivre…weren't wrong."

"…"

"I…broke…the promise I made to myself."

Her confession sounded like that of a holy woman who had committed a sin, reading back the charges against her. Her voice was clear, monotonous and dispirited, as it echoed under the moonlight. In her penitent admission, she wasn't castigating herself; there was only disappointment.

Aiz Wallenstein was unstable, more conflicted than even Riveria had ever seen her before.

A pained look crossed Riveria's face as she saw Aiz averting her eyes, cloaking herself in solitude. But moments later, the elf assumed the stance of the faction's second-in-command.

"Aiz. If you haven't made up your mind, I'll have you excluded from the plan for the upcoming assault on Knossos."

"!" Aiz's face snapped up.

Riveria pinned her with a stern gaze, making her announcement with a detached look. "Now that we have the key, the next plan will be a full-scale assault. An all-out war with the Evils. That's including the creatures. We don't have the freedom to bring along anyone who doesn't have the motivation to swing a sword."

"B-but…"

"It's true that the plan will be difficult to carry out without you. But more important is the fact that if you were struck down, it would have a major impact on the people in your unit."

As you are now, you would be a burden and nothing more. That was what Riveria was clearly telling her. Aiz could not say anything. She understood her current condition better than anyone. Even if she did take part in the fight, the way she was now, it would only lead to exactly the sort of situation Riveria was worried about. Aiz hung her head, trying to hide her disappointment.

"…Aiz, let me be honest," Riveria added, switching her tone

after she'd made her point as the second-in-command. She almost sounded like a mother. "Personally...I'm glad to see you're troubled by all this."

"...?"

"There's no right answer...You've begun to question the black flame that plagues you. You know, the path that you're on isn't all predetermined."

She stepped closer. In front of Aiz, who was curled up on top of the bed, Riveria met her golden gaze with jade eyes. Sitting down next to her, she gently brushed the girl's blond hair with her hand, gently admonishing her.

"Hesitate. Think. To your heart's content."

"..."

"And never forget: You aren't alone anymore...I'll say it as many times as I have to."

At that, Aiz opened her eyes wide for the first time.

She could feel the emotions behind that comment from Riveria, who had taken her under her wing. Finding herself embraced by Riveria's affection, Aiz felt the despair and insecurity that had latched onto her miraculously abate.

"...I...um...love you," added Riveria on what seemed to be a whim.

That left Aiz in even more shock than before.

Riveria seemed to realize she had said something astounding, because her cheeks became flushed, and she looked away. It was the kind of look that would normally never appear on her face. She seemed to be struggling with how to articulate her next thought, as if she was reluctant to say it, but she finally opened her mouth.

"I can't be your hero, but...I...You know."

From that, Aiz understood what Riveria was trying to tell her. Her desire to support Aiz made it through to her. It was funny to see Riveria acting so embarrassed, causing Aiz to break into a small smile. Her first one in a long while.

"Thank you, Riveria..." she replied on instinct.

She hadn't reached a decision on what to do with the hesitancy that still consumed her. But the difference between how she had been feeling before and now was night and day.

Aiz straightened, her body ready to move forward after standing still in the middle of the maze for so long, smiling like she had as a child. Riveria had been fidgeting, but when she saw that grin, the high elf stopped and kindly smiled back.

I have to get past doubting and worrying...

Aiz had not found an answer that could illuminate the darkness inside her. She might never find one. But she decided she'd had enough of sitting around doing nothing. When Aiz asked herself what she wanted to do now, it became simpler. She became honest with herself.

"Riveria...do you know what's happening to *Hestia Familia* now?"

"...? Their connection to the Xenos hasn't been made public. Right now, they should be behaving themselves until the situation dies down. After striking a deal with Ouranos's side, we have no plans to interact with them..."

Ever since the incident, Aiz had withdrawn into herself, which meant she did not have a clear grasp on the current situation in Orario.

Riveria looked puzzled as she explained it to her. "As for the hate aimed at Bell Cranell and the harm to his reputation, the commotion has mostly abated. I didn't see it myself, but apparently, his battle with the black minotaur swayed public opinion back in his favor."

"I see..." Aiz nodded in response, casting her gaze to the side, looking up at the dark sky and moon outside her window.

Aiz made her decision.

In order to resolve this doubt. In order to move forward. I have to see him.

It was before dawn, the time of morning when everything was still shrouded in darkness.

Beyond the city walls, the outline of the mountains was barely visible, covered in shadow. Past that shone a burst of crimson light. Lefiya had already woken up at this hour. More precisely, she had spotted a certain person through her window and scrambled down the halls of the manor in pursuit.

"...Miss Aiz."

She reached the midair hallway extending between towers. The blond-haired, golden-eyed girl was standing there, at the handrail, only looking forward as Lefiya saw her face in profile.

"Hey, Lefiya..."

"...What?"

Aiz wasn't brooding as she had been doing until yesterday. Instead, there was a freshness to her. Lefiya couldn't tell whether the morning air was this crisp in summer or something else was making her feel that way.

In either case, the elf felt as though she were standing before a spirit who would disappear if she reached out her hand.

"The armed monsters...I think they're called Xenos."

"Yes..."

"I think those monsters are...disgusting...No, I think that's what I want to think. In order to stop being confused. To be able to swing my sword."

"..."

"Lefiya...what do you think of them?"

Aiz shared her thoughts before asking her own question. It might well have been the first time Aiz had ever come to Lefiya seeking advice.

In their day-to-day lives, they relied on each other for small things, asked each other insignificant questions. But there had never been a time before when Aiz had truly asked her for her input.

The Sword Princess—more beautiful and stronger than anyone else—had come to her for help. And it made Lefiya both overjoyed and lonely to know that it had come at a time like this.

"...We..."

Lefiya started to respond but closed her mouth again. She was about to say, *We can't afford disunity in the familia right before the assault on Knossos*, but she stopped herself. Because this conversation had nothing to do with the fate of the city.

When she realized that Aiz was looking for her opinion as the elf Lefiya Viridis, she responded frankly, "I…I think those monsters are frightening, to tell you the truth. I think their very existence could turn the world as we know it upside down."

"…"

"That said, if there are people who would sacrifice themselves in order to plead on behalf of the Xenos…then I think we should lend those people an ear."

Lefiya couldn't bring herself to say she would have absolute trust or faith in the monsters. That was her honest opinion. As for the people trying to vouch for them…she would be open to believing in that boy. She'd seen him trying to protect the vouivre, even when it meant sustaining insult and injury. Lefiya believed it would be cowardly to shut her eyes and cover her ears whenever it would be more convenient to humanity that way. That was her opinion as someone who had herself been shaken by it.

Aiz must have been thinking about the same person. It was something that she really did not want to admit, but Lefiya had a hunch that was the case.

"…I see." After a long silence, Aiz nodded. Her beautiful golden hair fluttered, and the doubt that had been hanging about her face disappeared entirely. Lefiya's words had given her determination. The final push to make her decision. She felt extremely guilty about that.

"…I'm going out for a bit."

Turning her back, Aiz started to walk away. Lefiya did not try to ask where she was going.

"Okay…See you later."

She simply watched Aiz's back as she left.

She walked through the slumbering neighborhood, where no children were in sight, not after monsters had just emerged aboveground and thrown the city into an uproar. There were no adventurers drinking the night away or drunkards collapsed and dozing on the side of the road. As she savored the amusing thought that she might be the only person in the world, Aiz slipped through the quiet city by herself.

The sun started to rise. The eastern sky gradually lightened, turning blue near the horizon in the distance. By then, she'd reached her destination, the outer edge of Orario's northwest side, right in front of the towering city wall. Aiz ducked into the hidden entrance and climbed the long stairs before finally reemerging outside.

"..."

The wind was blowing. A morning breeze coming in from the east. The figure of a single adventurer was standing there, bathed in the morning glow. White hair and rubellite eyes. The boy was still, gazing at the stark white tower in the center of the city.

"Miss Aiz...?"

"Yes...Good morning."

As Aiz silently approached, the boy—Bell—had noticed her.

"...Why are you here?"

"I'm not sure...I guess I thought if I came, I might find you."

That was the truth. After witnessing his fight with the black minotaur and talking with Riveria, she suspected that the boy before her would come here, to the top of the city wall. This was the place where he had tried to get stronger, driven on by his countless training sessions with Aiz.

"I see."

"Mm-hmm."

"..."

"..."

A blank space was accompanied by extended silence. But this wasn't an uncomfortable passage of time.

The wind rustled their hair.

"Miss Aiz."

"?"

"Will you teach me how to fight again?"

"...Even after what happened?"

"Yes." There was no doubt in his eyes as he nodded.

The magnificent chalk-white tower piercing the sky—and the labyrinth slumbering below it.

It brought to mind promises and conclusions.

Aiz felt just left behind in that moment. By someone who was still far weaker, by the boy who should have been looking up at a goal that was too high, too far beyond his reach.

"…You're a sly one."

"…I'm sorry."

That's why Aiz said what she was really thinking.

"…Fine."

"…Really?"

"Yes…You have the same eyes."

"?"

"The ones I always see in the mirror." But Aiz was relieved. "Yes… But they're different…They're not strange like mine. They're more beautiful, and, um."

"…*Pfft.*"

"…What are you laughing about?"

"I-I'm sorry."

Because despite branching out on their own paths and crossing blades, their bond had not been severed.

"I…have some things to take care of, so I'm not sure when I can do it."

"That's okay…Thank you."

"Not at all."

"…"

"…"

"Miss Aiz."

"What?"

And then he said it.

"I…want to become stronger."

That struck Aiz's heart to her core in its current state.

"…Really?"

"Yes."

"I'm going now."

"Okay."

"…See you."

"…Okay."

Turning away, she started to walk. For once, Aiz did not turn around to watch him go as she felt him getting farther away. She only looked forward—toward the place that she needed to go, marching on the path she had chosen.

"I…want to become stronger, too."

From their meeting, Aiz reaped that phrase—it wasn't an answer. She still hadn't found a way to escape the woods where she had gotten lost. But it had inspired something in her. That boy had decided on his journey, and she renewed her determination to forge ahead, too, so that she would not get left behind.

"It…was good that I met you now."

He's going to start sprinting forward again. That's why I'll start running, too. Overcome my doubts. For now.

I…should learn from him, she thought, assuming this frame of mind: his approach to becoming strong, no matter what the appearances. That was something she needed now. She had to become stronger—in order to defeat Knossos, in order to avoid losing to that red-haired creature again.

Descending the stairs from the city wall, Aiz came out at a dash—not heading toward Twilight Manor in the north but to the south, where a certain *strongest* one resided.

CHAPTER 2

THE DECISIVE
BATTLE
INTERMISSION

Гэта казка іншага сям'і,

бітва антрактам

The sun had cleared the horizon, peeking over the city wall.

By the time the city began to rouse its heavy eyelids as it stirred awake and the morning bustle gradually started to spread, Aiz had reached Orario's southern area in the Fifth District.

Rising before her was a towering gate and four walls that were a bit too solid to call a fence. Despite being in the middle of Orario's most lively and varied Shopping District, it boasted the appearance of a castle wall. There was no guard at the gate, just a tense atmosphere, like the calm before a storm. It was probably a warning to all not to approach.

Which Aiz did not heed. She came to a halt, looking up and walking in front of the gate. With a completely serious look, demonstrating her resolve, she banged it with her fist as if knocking on a door.

"...I'm coming for thee."

Bam! Bam! echoed a silly sound unbefitting a majestic gate.

According to Loki, that was what people were supposed to say when announcing a martial arts challenge—er, knocking on the gate of someone else's home. *Well, it should be fine.* That's what she believed, standing there with a comically earnest look on her face. She did not realize that in this situation, it was the kind of fatal misunderstanding that would have scared the hell out of even Loki, who would have foamed at the mouth.

Before long, the doors opened with a weighty creak.

"..."

Aiz sauntered forward and through the gate, where upon she found a green wilderness spreading before her eyes. Small white and golden rings of flowers rippled in a beautiful field that one would not expect to see in the middle of a city. The field was covered by flowers that could be crushed by a single step, and the land was lush.

And in the middle of the field, at the heart of the estate, was a hill. Atop that was a giant manor that could be mistaken for a temple or palace. The magnificent sight carefully isolated from the complex cityscape around it could almost be a painting.

Aiz was captivated as she stepped into a place that she had never been in before, while the gate groaned loudly again, shutting behind her.

"!"

In an instant, she was surrounded. A swarm of adventurers appeared all at once, from above and behind cover. Forming a ring around Aiz, they all held weapons, and every last one of those weapons was pointed at her. Their perfect encirclement was almost artistic, speaking volumes to their level of training. At the same time, a dangerous hostility was brewing beneath the surface.

"—Marching in here by yourself, huh? You looking to start something?"

Ringed by a multitude of weapons, Aiz was assailed by a rough voice that made no attempt to hide its malice. A single animal person emerged from the group surrounding her: a male cat person with black and silver fur, incredibly intimidating despite being considerably shorter than Aiz.

Aiz remembered him. He was one of the assassins who had attacked under the cover of darkness after one of her training sessions on the wall with that boy. At the time, his face had been concealed by a visor and he'd been equipped with night-raid gear, but now he was wearing standard battle clothes, leaving his sharp eyes and features on display.

His title was Vana Freya and his name was Allen Fromel. The very model of a first-tier adventurer.

"What do you want, doll girl?"

The name of that place was Folkvangr.

Home of *Freya Familia*.

"If you have something to say, you've got two seconds. If you just want to die, then keep standing there with your mouth shut."

She was curtly told that questions would not be tolerated.

Allen's sharp gaze pierced through Aiz, who was hemmed in by a thick curtain of tension that was completely at odds with the clear blue sky and sunlight streaming in from above.

No, it certainly wasn't just Allen. The other adventurers, the members of *Freya Familia*, were glaring at her with hostility, as if they were preparing to avenge a slain parent. From their point of view, one of the core members of a hostile faction had appeared without warning in the early morning, meaning their response was understandable, but—

...That's weird. I made sure to say "I'm coming for thee," following the proper protocol when you visit someone... Then why...?

Ever the airhead in these sorts of situations, Aiz was completely lost.

I followed Loki's instructions to a T, but I'm somehow a half step away from a fight to the death. Did I get something wrong? Or did you trick me, Loki?

A cold sweat beaded on her cheek. The younger version of herself residing in her heart had grown distant following the incident with the dragon girl, but at the moment, her inner child was contorting herself in a weird pose, holding her hands together in prayer.

Aiz had no idea what she should do even as her agitation mounted under the mask of a composed expression that hid her emotions. She wasn't able to say anything in response.

"All right. Death it is."

It had been exactly two seconds.

Paying no heed to Aiz's situation, Allen thrust his silver spear with blinding speed. He was about to skewer the defenseless girl before she could even draw her sword.

"—What's going on?"

But just before he could stab her, a sonorous voice echoed across the field like the strumming of a harp. Aiz's eyes focused on the source—directly ahead of her, atop the hill. She looked at the figure descending the white stairs extending from the manor. Though they were some distance away from each other, the owner of the voice exuded the gravitas of a queen as she approached them with a single attendant in tow.

In an instant, all the adventurers surrounding Aiz assumed a reverent stance, like faithful retainers. But their caution toward Aiz did not waver in the slightest, which was to be expected. Allen was the only one who didn't move, continuing to keep his spear right in front of Aiz's eyes as the patron goddess of the city's greatest familia, Freya, approached them.

"I thought it seemed a bit noisy, but…hee-hee-hee, if a rare guest has paid us a visit, I suppose it's only natural."

Freya's robe covered everything except her face. She must have been planning to depart early in the morning, considering that if the Goddess of Beauty went out into the city without any disguise, it would cause a commotion. When Aiz glanced behind her, she could see a carriage waiting beside the gate. That might have been another reason why the response to her visit had been so dramatic.

"I'm sorry for allowing you to see this eyesore, Lady Freya. I'll have it cleaned up in no time."

"It's fine, Allen. Lower your spear."

"There's no need for that. I'll just cut her throat right now."

"Allen."

"…"

Freya smiled as she spoke his name. That was all it took for the rabid dog—er, *cat* to slowly lower his spear. Possessing incredible charisma, Freya was revered by her followers as though she were a queen—an idol that must be protected at all costs. Her orders were absolute. Freya turned her gaze to Aiz, ignoring the cat person who was clearly venting his displeasure, though he obediently lowered his spear.

"And what do you want, Sword Princess?"

"…I'd like…to ask a favor."

"You have a favor to ask? Of us? Oh-ho, that's odd. And just what might that be?"

Freya looked genuinely curious. The smile of a child crossed her face. At the goddess's urging, Aiz looked away from Freya, fixing her eyes on someone behind her—at the solitary boaz standing back, attending to her. At the one who had desired the title of the city's strongest while, at the same time, standing at its pinnacle.

The Warlord, Ottar. As the warrior's rust-colored eyes watched her intently, Aiz lowered her head.

"Please train with me."

The wind whistled, an invisible breeze passing through the beautiful field.

Ottar opened his eyes wide. Allen's movements ground to a halt. Even Freya's silver eyes flickered with surprise. Every other familia member was astonished. Blowing away all of *Freya Familia*, Aiz continued to gaze fixedly at the grass at her feet, keeping her head down.

"Heh…hee-hee-hee!" Freya was the first to make a sound, of course.

Though she covered her mouth, a giggle slipped past her fingers, sounding like a songbird's chirps. The next to speak was Allen, who could not keep his annoyance under wraps anymore.

"Just how stupid are you? Who the hell would be dumb enough to train an asshole from an enemy familia? Argh! Screw it all! Die!"

His scathing response was entirely on point.

Aiz raised her head. Rather than trying to explain herself, she was forthcoming, spilling the feelings in her heart—not to Allen or to Freya but to the warrior.

"I…can't lose anymore. No. I don't want to lose. Not to that person, that creature…If I lose against them, I might lose everything."

"…"

"That's why…I want to become stronger."

But that wasn't enough of an explanation for someone who did not know about the existence of Knossos or the creature she referred to. It could have been a complete non sequitur.

But there was a tenacity in her voice permeating each word, and that was very real.

"Even Finn and the others couldn't win against them."

"…"

"I don't know anyone stronger than me—stronger than them… except you. That's why I want to learn from you."

Allen's cheek twitched. Even Aiz could tell he was itching to kill her. She knew full well that she was shamelessly asking for a huge favor. And that by doing this, she might be betraying Finn and the others. But when Aiz had heard Bell say that he wanted to become stronger, she decided to throw away all concern about appearances or obligations.

In order to beat Knossos. In order to defeat the creature Levis.

*I want to become stronger, too…*Lifting her head, she repeated that to herself.

She had returned to her starting point, embracing the pure original intent she'd had when she first took up her sword. As expected, she could not tell what the city's strongest adventurer was thinking as she looked at him. But unlike the other familia members, he accepted Aiz's resolve with a tranquil face—as if he was the only person in the world who understood her.

"—Very well. I'll allow it."

But there was another one who acknowledged her: the goddess watching Aiz.

"Lady Freya."

Allen's eyes flashed, as did those of the other familia members. Of course they did. Their faction and Aiz's were the two heads of the city, the most powerful familias and each other's greatest rivals. And Freya was allowing them to train that rival. There was no reason to give Aiz that.

Allen had raised his voice not in simple agitation—but in open anger. It was enough that Aiz started to feel extraordinarily embarrassed. But Freya paid his pointed glare no mind as she looked into Aiz's eyes.

"Sword Princess, just to confirm, your goal has to do with the assault on Knossos, right?"

"…Yes." She was flustered when she heard Freya say the word *Knossos*, but she managed to nod.

The goddess could see in her eyes that Aiz wasn't lying. Freya's smile deepened before she looked back at Allen, who was the lone voice of dissent.

"Like Loki said. If I act like everything's fine, we might end up at a point that's beyond salvation. There's no sense regretting it all if I only do it after Orario disappears," Freya capriciously continued. "Allen? I don't want to become the kind of queen who would act the way Loki described. Or would you all rather fight alongside Loki's children?"

"...I'd rather die."

"Then wouldn't it be easier to cooperate?"

That shut him up, though he was visibly angry, showing the signs of an ill-tempered cat who might someday turn his claws on his master.

However, in the end, Allen did not say anything.

"Ottar, do you mind?"

"If you allow it, Lady Freya, then...I'm willing to accept it as an adventurer."

Freya seemed satisfied by his response as she nodded. Aiz watched with bated breath as she waited to see how it would go.

Just as she was nervously starting to think that she might have somehow succeeded, Freya suddenly leaned in.

"But! I can't just let this happen for free."

"...!"

"Allen made a fair point. We have to be sufficiently compensated..."

Aiz was shaken by the unexpected response as Freya's face loomed closer to hers. The goddess's eyes narrowed as she placed a finger on Aiz's chin, lifting her head.

"Let's make a contract, Sword Princess."

"A...contract...?"

"Yes. I'll lend you Ottar and let him train you. In exchange, you'll owe us a favor."

"..."

"No need to eye me so suspiciously. The debt will be repaid whenever, however, and with whatever I decide. But I won't demand anything unreasonable. Or at least nothing more unreasonable than what you are asking for now. I swear on my name," Freya added sweetly into Aiz's ear.

With a gaze that could entrance even a deity, she trained her eyes on Aiz, who was transfixed.

Aiz did not know what the goddess was thinking. And she couldn't think of any way she could pay back a debt to someone who had everything. However, it was an acceptable trade. Or at least, it should have been.

Aiz gritted her teeth as she returned Freya's gaze, as if resisting her allure.

"…As long as it's only a personal debt…and does not involve my familia…"

Aiz somehow managed to wring out that last condition. Freya smiled and nodded, her dainty finger letting go of Aiz's chin, standing back up to meet her gaze. Aiz instinctively clasped her hand to her neck. For some reason, she felt like a collar had just been slipped around it, even though there was nothing there.

Without realizing it, the girl with golden hair and golden eyes and the goddess with silver hair and silver eyes had finalized a contract.

"Oh my, look at the time. I have to get going. Ottar, I'll leave the rest to you."

"Yes, my lady. But…for your attendant…"

"I'll take Helen."

Accompanied by a single female familia member, Freya climbed into the waiting carriage. As though she'd already lost interest in Aiz, the goddess disappeared through the open gate without a single glance back.

Once Freya had left and he was freed of his obligations as her attendant, Ottar walked up to Aiz and peered down at her.

"…As you requested, I'll cross swords with you. Are you ready?"

"Yes." With her beloved sword Desperate at her hip, Aiz nodded without a trace of doubt in her eyes.

"All of you are forbidden to speak of this. This is a secret agreement forged between our lady and the Sword Princess. I will not tolerate it becoming fodder for vulgar rumors. What happens in Folkvangr stays in Folkvangr."

""Sir!""

With the air of a brusque commander, Ottar gave the familia members a strict order. Though they were in a disorderly array after their patron goddess had left, they all acknowledged his order as one.

In the midst of that, only one, just Allen, turned his back to the others with visible rage.

Ottar called out to him as he started to return to the manor. "Allen, you help, too."

"Don't go ordering me around, asshole. You two can just do whatever the hell you want."

Ottar silently watched as the cat person made no attempt to hide his distaste, walking away.

As for Aiz, it was brought to her attention again that she'd made an absurd request, which was making her feel slightly uncomfortable.

"Nonetheless…" Ottar's voice suddenly had a different tone to it. "I'm surprised Finn and his crew are letting you do this."

"………"

Ottar was genuinely impressed. Aiz quietly averted her eyes as she struggled to control the sweat forming on her brow.

—*What do I do? I didn't tell them anything.*

"Apparently, Aiz has started going off to train by herself," Riveria said as she looked down at the unfurled scroll—a letter addressed to her.

The location was *Loki Familia*'s home, Twilight Manor. Two days had passed since the leaders had announced the deal they had made with the Xenos. Thanks to the work done by Raul, Anakity, and the other second-string team members, the familia was finally in the process of reaching a consensus when Aiz had suddenly disappeared without a trace. The letter in Riveria's hands had just come in, providing an explanation.

"She was in bad spirits, and I was starting to think we might have to leave her out of the plan as Riveria proposed, but…seems she was able to right herself," Finn commented.

"And training at this time means she must be back to herself. Ga-ha-ha-ha!" Gareth added.

"That's Mama Riveria for ya!" Loki chimed in.

"I certainly did talk to her…but I've no idea how she got the idea of going to train into her mind."

Ignoring their responses, Riveria looked conflicted as she gazed down at the letter in her hands, which said: *please don't look for me i'm traning in secret*, written in a very shaky hand. That misspelling. The scattered inkblots. It all spoke to the intensity of the special training, given the fact that she didn't even have the energy to properly hold a quill.

Riveria's shapely brows furrowed, but…she had heard from the receptionist Misha Frot that Aiz had delivered it to Guild Headquarters herself. Plus, she'd added that "she looked super beat-up and uber-tired!" But Riveria imagined she was fine, taking that account as evidence of a vigorous training session. She decided the young adventurer had to be holed up somewhere in the Dungeon.

"In any case, the last bit of concern has been cleared up," Finn said as he looked down at the desk set up in the middle of the room.

Riveria, Gareth, and Loki followed suit, directing their attention to the maps and a strategic document with an array of information enumerated on it sprawled across the desk.

Since they had announced the deal with the Xenos, no one had withdrawn from the mission. *Loki Familia* had mustered the resolve to swallow that pill and take on the assault of Knossos.

"It helps that we managed to get a map from Riveria's surprise attack. You knocked out one of the monster plants, too, right?"

"Still, the map only covers a small piece of the enormous labyrinth. And there's no way that plant was the last of them. We should assume the enemy still has extant forces ready to fight and keep in mind that they hold a significant territorial advantage."

"You're right, Riveria, but we also have information from when

Gareth and I went in. I'll summarize the basic outline of the plan, including all of that."

In the strategy meeting for the leadership, there was an energetic exchange of opinions and confirmation of information. But Finn was still the mainstay of the strategic efforts.

"First of all, we have multiple keys in our possession. Counting the ones the Xenos have—which should be considered Ouranos's side—we have five of them. We need to make the most of all five in order to advance the attack."

The first was the Daedalus Orb that Anakity had stolen with Lilly's help. The second was the one Riveria had managed to capture inside Knossos. The third was the one that Hermes had exchanged with Cruz and his squad in the underground passage—the one that Freya had secretly been keeping. And the remaining two were the ones the Xenos had in their possession.

With Loki looking on as an adviser, the prum leader put into words the strategy he had sketched out in his head.

"In order to plan an assault, we need a complete map of the interior of Knossos," he said as he tapped the map Rakuta had created, which was spread out across the desk. "All passages, as well as an escape route in the worst case. And most importantly, the optimal path to sneak in directly to our target. If we can't get at least that much, then eradicating the demi-spirit will be very difficult."

Next to the map were rough sketches that Finn had drawn: the demi-spirit they had faced on the fifty-ninth floor of the Dungeon and the one Gareth had fought with the others during their first venture into Knossos. They were a plant-type monster and a bull-type monster. They looked just like what Riveria and Gareth remembered. Next to the pictures were means of attack, weak points, and other detailed characteristics.

Their highest priority was killing the demi-spirit that could invoke the destruction of Orario.

"Knossos has dangerous traps. If at all possible, I'd like to neutralize those, too."

"The more I hear, the more time and work it sounds like it's going to take…"

"Don't forget people, too. Knossos reaches all the way down to the Dungeon's middle levels. I thought I was ready for it, but…"

Gareth and Riveria groaned at the scale of the enemy's base, which precluded ordinary methods of assault. Based on what they had learned from Ouranos's allies and from Ikelos, who had been cast out of the city, it was confirmed that Knossos reached all the way to the eighteenth floor. It would be impossible for *Loki Familia* to clear it by themselves. That was exactly why they were planning to fight alongside the Xenos.

Ignoring their complaints, Finn touched upon the core of his strategy. "That's why—I've split the operation into two stages."

Riveria and Gareth were thunderstruck. Loki whistled in amusement.

"The first attack is to get a comprehensive understanding of the layout of Knossos. And the second is to eliminate our targets after determining the optimal route. You could call the former a reconnaissance in force, which would make the latter an all-out, decisive battle."

Finn laid out the theory behind the strategy and its objectives. The former would eliminate the enemy forces and any other impediments while concurrently mapping the lay of the land. The latter would be just as described: breaching the enemy's bastion and destroying the demi-spirit using everything they had gleaned from the first probing attack.

The dwarf and high elf felt the weight of their objectives.

"A bold method you picked there. If the enemy can finish their preparations, or rather, if they can finish summoning the demi-spirit aboveground, then that's basically it for us…Isn't this a race against time?"

"No. During the fight on Daedalus Street, Aki gathered some information from the enemy's detached force when she took the key. They didn't know details of the plan, but even in the worst case, it seems like the beginning of their plan for the demi-spirit won't be ready for at least twenty days. Which means we still have a bit of leeway."

"I see...What ended up happening to the captured prisoners?"

"*Committed suicide.* Apparently, one of them was a curse user... He sacrificed his body in exchange for creating a powerful curse that killed the others right in front of our familia members' eyes. These enemies aren't afraid of death...No, they're true believers who trust in their covenant with Thanatos, completely willing to die... These are some extremely twisted people."

Riveria could not contain her disgust as she explained the fate of the prisoners who had been captured. Gareth grimaced as Finn decided to get the conversation back on track.

"In any event, while we have some wiggle room, we don't have time to take it easy. Depending on when we can complete the first assault, we need to be ready to quickly shift gears and launch the second."

"Fiiiinn? Are you *sure* you want the first attack to just be the initial setup and the second plan to be when we take care of the targets?" Loki drawled.

"Yeah. If we get a chance to take out one of the targets during the first one, then we should try. We'll play it by ear, but...if something equivalent to the demi-spirit on the fifty-ninth floor has already emerged, then normal adventurers won't be able to deal with it. To be absolutely sure, I want to preserve as much of our forces as possible for the second attack," Finn responded as he met Loki's vermilion eyes. "Which is why, if at all possible, I'd like to use the Guild to recruit troops."

"Working together with other familias? Well, the situation and the whole 'the fate of the city's at stake' shtick might sound kinda laughable, but there's no good reason not to get help from other people."

Loki was forced to agree that, tragically, this was not something *Loki Familia* could handle alone. Riveria and Gareth both nodded in agreement.

"My guess is that Fei-Fei and Ganesha might help after understanding the situation. And I'm forcing Hermes to join this time. That familia is light on their feet—the right fit for the mapping job."

"It sounded like he was pulling a lot of strings during the mess with the Xenos. Can we trust him?"

"Not much farther than we can throw him, but there's no way he would pull something to screw this up. Even he wouldn't go that far."

"*Freya Familia*...There's not much point in expecting anything there, huh?"

"Yeah. Even if we told them about the danger to the city, they would never just obediently cooperate. They'll only move according to Freya's divine will or her whims."

"We should ditch that stupid pervert and make her a loner. The empress in new clothes. When it's all said and done, we can make fun of her as much as we want."

"Ha-ha-ha...That reminds me, Loki. I want to ask *Dian Cecht Familia* for help, too. That one can be in the form of a quest, though."

Even after she left the administrative stuff to the Guild, Loki frequently ended up having to settle discussions with the patron gods in other familias, which was why she started making a list of all the potential familias for this job while the others talked. With this situation, they didn't need to inform any more familias than necessary. If it leaked that the remnants of the Evils were planning something, the city would fall into a panic. The residents of Orario still remembered the Dark Ages of the city, when evil abounded.

"...It was like this back when the Evils were running strong, too, but managing relations among familias are difficult. Even though a clear and present danger faces the city, it's hard for everyone to work together to deal with it."

Riveria suddenly compared the current situation to the Dark Ages, which had lasted until five years ago.

The problem was that the deities weren't cut from the same cloth. Some factions, *Freya Familia* being the obvious example, would never work together without some sort of official reason, and they were frustratingly slow when they finally did move out.

"No use in lamenting it now. We just have to do what needs to be done."

Switching topics, Finn focused back on the planning for the first strike.

"I said I wanted to preserve forces for the second attack, but obviously our familia will have to participate in both parts. It's our plan, after all. And we're the only ones who have any experience with everything that Knossos can bring to bear."

He made it clear contextually that they would have to take the role of guides leading mixed squads as he explained the actual details of the operation.

"We touched on it earlier, but we need numbers for the first attack, not quality—the manpower to be able to map a labyrinth rivaling the Dungeon."

"Dividing into multiple squads to attack...ultra-human-wave tactics."

"Yes. There's no shortcut here. We're going to use this attack to get ahold of the best route to clear out Knossos, just like all our predecessors who mapped the route through the Dungeon."

"The goal?" Gareth asked.

"Eighty percent. Worst case, seventy," Finn responded, dumbfounding Gareth.

"Mapping over seventy percent of that giant maze...To be honest, I'm a bit dizzy just imagining doing it."

"In order to be able to finish things with the second assault, that's what we'll need to accomplish. Well, there is one other shortcut we could use...but that's something we should leave to the likes of *Hermes Familia*."

Finn shrugged when Gareth winced. It was then that Riveria finally brought up the biggest point of concern.

"And what will we do about the creature?"

That still needed to be handled: the redheaded woman Levis.

"In order to achieve your goals, it seems reasonable to think it will be a drawn-out fight...That'll take time. And the more time we give that creature, the greater the risk for our forces."

"..."

Of all the enemy pieces, Levis would undoubtedly be the queen.

She was a powerful unit that could move in every direction. Her attack signaled death to all who encountered her.

In order to finish the map, they would resort to the brute-force method of human-wave tactics, but precisely because they were spread out, any squad faced with Levis would be unable to deal with her. Choosing to disperse their forces greatly increased the odds of their attack ending in a defeat where each squad was crushed one by one.

On top of that, there was currently no method of tracking Levis's individual movements and mustering sufficient force to deal with her inside that giant labyrinth. The battle would turn into a stalemate, increasing the overall damage sustained by their forces.

Finn pursed his lips.

"...Are you planning to carry out this strategy while accepting the costs?" Riveria asked, lowering her voice.

The implication was: *Will you sacrifice our allies in order to achieve the objective?*

"*I've no intention of abandoning anyone,*" he responded clearly. "I won't accept the loss of people on this mission. If a squad gets wiped out, all the mapping they achieved will be wasted. To say nothing of problems with morale. If we allow the creature to run free, our allies will be crushed in the blink of an eye."

"...!"

"I'm not planning a fight under the assumption that we'll be taking any losses. We're not going to sacrifice anyone to that creature."

Riveria and Gareth both gazed in wonder at his response. Loki stopped moving, her lips curling up.

He didn't say as much, but Finn made it clear he was searching for a solution that involved no losses at all, not just one that minimized them.

The old Finn Deimne would have simply made the sacrifice without any doubt. To overcome the reality of the situation, he would never have chased after ideals in the first place. He would have made every effort to control the situation and keep losses to the lowest possible level. But Finn had abandoned that assumption.

It wasn't that he had suddenly become overly optimistic about their chances. It was simply an expression of his resolve to achieve his ideals. He had his eyes on a much more difficult path than simply accepting losses as a necessary cost of victory.

As a realist, Finn now had the bravery to smash the scales. He was no longer someone who wanted to accept sacrificing his allies with a cold heart.

Riveria and Gareth understood that it was the result of the answer he had come to during the incident with the Xenos. But it was also a dazzling thing to behold.

When all was said and done, Finn was still the youngest member of the familia's commanders. At times like this, Riveria and Gareth shared the sort of happiness that a parent might have watching their child growing up. Loki smiled in satisfaction, as if welcoming Finn's transformation.

"If Aiz can take part in the plan, then I have a plan for dealing with this creature. Can you leave that to me for the time being?" Finn asked with a resolute gaze.

Riveria and Gareth both smiled, entrusting it to him. Finn appeared even more reliable than before as he continued explaining his strategy for the attack. Pointing to the map and rough sketches of the monsters on the desktop, he precisely covered the main points.

"For the time being, there are some critical things that we have to gather. Without those, we can't carry out the plan."

"The secret anti-curse medicine?"

"Yeah. The fighting will be extremely intense starting with the very first assault. We'll need to have resources to deal with the unhealable curse."

The soldiers inside Knossos were equipped with cursed weapons. Amid's medicine was the only thing capable of dispelling the afflictions they caused, which made it indispensable.

"If we mess this up and fail, we lose everything, so we will set aside enough time until the operation begins. But in the meantime, we'll harass Knossos."

The enemy had shut themselves up inside Knossos, meaning

they were essentially holing up to wait out the siege. It allowed *Loki Familia* ample opportunity to put the pressure on their enemy: for example, starving the enemy of supplies or launching intermittent attacks when they were least expecting them. There were likely more paths connected to the Dungeon that *Loki Familia* did not know about yet, but if they placed an inspection at Babel, then the Knossos forces would not be able to reach the surface. At best, they would only be able to scavenge for what little food could be found inside the Dungeon. Finn's plan involved working with *Ganesha Familia* to create a tight net.

"For the first attack, I'd like us and *Hermes Familia* to participate. And after that, I'd like to call on a familia with lots of members to help, but..." Trailing off, Finn suddenly looked to his patron goddess. "Loki, what about *Dionysus Familia*?"

The other member of their alliance was *Dionysus Familia*. The members of that familia were undeniably lacking in level and strength, but they boasted quantity. They were the ideal familia to help with the mapping.

Loki paused for a few beats before responding. "...Let's put that on hold for now."

"Why? This isn't the time to be tripping one another up, trying to read one another's motives. Now that the big thing that Ouranos was hiding has been cleared up, Dionysus should have no reason to be on guard against the Guild."

Loki did not respond to the question that Riveria hurled into the mix.

Watching the silent goddess for a bit, Finn responded, "All right, I guess. We can leave this to Loki," changing the topic.

And then he revealed their critical partners for this mission.

"I'm planning to have them, the Xenos, join the first attack."

"A double envelopment from Daedalus Street and the eighteenth floor, huh...?" Fels repeated to confirm.

Ouranos responded "Yes" with a solemn nod.

They were in the Chamber of Prayers beneath Guild Headquarters. Atop the altar, surrounded by four burning torches, Ouranos and Fels were looking at the document from *Loki Familia*.

"The adventurers and the Xenos are to operate in separate groups without merging, huh…So the Xenos will attack from the eighteenth floor, and the adventurers will come in from aboveground…Braver sure is a fast worker. There's not much more reassuring than having him as an ally."

Organizing the adventurers and Xenos in separate groups was ideal to avoid any mishaps due to the adventurers' lingering hatred of monsters. While he was attempting to achieve the ideal outcome, Braver was by no means willing to blindly trust in ideals alone. In addition, the document indicated that Fels was to take command of the Xenos's side. Finn was counting on the mage's skill. A hint of a sigh leaked out from Fels's jet-black robes at that.

"I can accept this proposal. And you, Ouranos?"

"No objection."

"Then I'll offer them oculi. If we're able to communicate inside Knossos, that will increase the precision of the mapping for this first stage."

The mage took out a crystal capable of conveying sight and sound that could fit in the palm of a hand. Entrusting them with such a valuable magic item was proof of Fels's trust in them and expressed the mage's resolve to defeat the people hiding away inside that labyrinth.

"Fels, how much of the Xenos's fighting force can take part?"

"About thirty of them, including Lido, Rei, and Gros. However, it seems the minotaur could not be stopped and immediately went down to the deep levels. There is no telling when he will return, so we can't count on him for this first attack."

The pitch-black minotaur had been officially categorized as Level 7 by the Guild. Though disappointed that they would not be able to make use of his strength for this mission, Fels changed gears without getting hung up on it.

Even if it was just this once for the sake of the assault on Knossos, the fact that Finn had requested this secret pact meant there was no reason to hold back anymore. They would join hands with *Loki Familia* without hesitation in order to protect the city.

As they were speaking, a new shadow approached the altar.

"Yo, in the middle of strategizing? From the looks of it, you seem to be working together with Loki and them."

"God Hermes…"

Ouranos glanced at the god who emerged, and Fels turned to face him.

"Whew, that's a load off my mind. It always felt like I was having to play the part of a double agent before."

"…"

"Now Loki will stop being so suspicious of me, and this can end without me getting an ulcer," the god announced with a hint of sarcasm as he removed his hat. That it did not sound unpleasant was perhaps because he genuinely was relieved.

In truth, during the Xenos incident, he had essentially been acting as a double agent. But they valued his work chasing after the Evils' Remnants, which was why they weren't blaming him for forming an alliance with Loki and them. Other than the part where he had gone off on his own to try to cover up the Xenos.

Fels recoiled a bit, as if not particularly pleased with Hermes for acting out of line during the struggle on Daedalus Street. But as would be expected, Ouranos showed no sign of agitation.

"…There are a few things I'd like to say, but, God Hermes, might I inquire as to why you have an imprint of a foot on your face? It appears almost as if you got drop-kicked there. And with perfect form, no less…" Fels said, rather suspicious.

"Ha-ha-ha. You should read the vibe and realize that's not the sort of thing you should be asking. It's neither here nor there, but let's just call it taking responsibility for things with a certain young goddess." The suave god with a distinct red mark on his face feigned a laugh.

"What business do you have, Hermes?"

"Hmm. I guess the god who created this city isn't a fan of small talk. Okay, then allow me to get right to it." Hermes's mood suddenly turned serious. "I suspect the assault on Knossos will happen in the near future, but…I want to keep young Bell—*Hestia Familia*—far away from it."

Fels looked surprised, but Hermes paid the mage no heed as he continued.

"He took another step forward during the fight in the Labyrinth District. One great enough to overcome my divine will and make a fool of me. I don't want him to get wrapped up in this brutal fight right after he managed to reach a new stage of development. At the very least, *not yet*."

The Guild had already publicly announced that Bell Cranell had reached Level 4. Hermes's proposal was out of respect for the boy's lightning-fast progress, as if he didn't want anything to dim his radiance.

Fels and Ouranos had stopped moving. They did not reject Hermes. Instead, they seemed to agree with him, accepting his proposal.

"Very well. We had no intention of forcing more of a load onto Bell Cranell after his assistance with the Xenos incident."

"But even if you want him distanced from it, how exactly would you suggest we do that, God Hermes?"

"Give *Hestia Familia* a mission to go on an expedition. That should be sufficient. With his level-up, their familia rank should be a D, which means they now have a duty to help clear the Dungeon," Hermes responded effortlessly.

He was suggesting that they head into the Dungeon for the period of time when Ouranos's and Loki's forces were working together to take on Knossos in their large-scale operation.

"I think it is a bit hasty, since they only just went up in rank, but… the Guild seems to have high expectations of *Hestia Familia*, too. It should be acceptable to outside observers. Very well. I'll pull some strings."

"I'm counting on you."

Finishing the conversation about the boy, Ouranos returned to the main topic. "Hermes, what will you do about the plan to attack Knossos?"

"My familia will be taking part, of course. Well, more like neither Loki nor you guys would let me hang back even if I tried to sit this one out."

Hermes shrugged, and then his orange eyes narrowed.

"It's been a roundabout path, but we're finally reaching the end. We're going to unmask whoever Enyo is with this battle."

Enyo.

In the words of the gods, it meant *the destroyer of cities*: the mysterious person who had plotted the destruction of Orario and brought together the Evils' Remnants, the corrupted spirit, and other underground forces. The instigator of the current situation and the one they suspected of being its mastermind.

"I'll leave the flashy parts of the attack plan to *Loki Familia* and the Xenos. Leave the skulking around in the shadows behind the scenes to my kids…in order to track down all the clues we can find."

Hermes pulled a chess piece from his cloak. A black king—Enyo. He rolled it around the palm of his hand before clenching his fist. With Knossos surrounded, they had their opponents in check. And they would keep moving forward until they reached checkmate. Hermes had lost some of his own children in the course of all this, and the intent of his divine will was blazing in his eyes.

Ouranos and Fels responded with silent assent.

"So when will the attack begin? There's a lot to prepare for the final plan, right?"

Returning to his aloof tone, he glanced over at the letter in Fels's hands. Looking down at the document spelling out the key points of Finn's plan, the black-robed mage responded.

"The anticipated start date is—"

"L-L-Level Four…! H-h-h-he caught up to me…?!"

With her whole body trembling, Lefiya gripped the notice sheet declaring a certain adventurer's level-up. Printed on the sheet was the white-haired boy's likeness, along with an extensive report on the official announcement of his expedition mission.

"What's Lefiya on about?"

"I think she's just happy about Argonaut leveling up!"

Tione looked puzzled as Lefiya held the paper in front of her face and quivered at high speed while Tiona laughed loudly. The elf had been worried about Aiz, and the Amazon was mistaking her current mood, assuming she was feeling less down. Ignoring the Amazon's misunderstanding, she felt the shock as it made her quake.

"—I see you are all here."

Suddenly, Riveria appeared. They were in the manor's dining hall.

There had been an announcement that there was important news to be shared, so almost everyone, from the elites down to the lowest-level members, was gathered there. Aiz was the only one absent.

"We've ironed out all the pieces of the strategy for the attack on Knossos. Make sure you don't miss anything I'm about to say."

Finn was busy gathering all the necessary pieces, which was why Riveria stood before everyone in his stead to share the details of the plan. The familia members listened closely with serious, almost menacing looks on their faces.

"Riveria, when is it going to start?"

Tiona raised her hand and asked without reading the vibe of the room.

Riveria nodded.

"The operation will begin—in ten days' time."

CHAPTER 3

THE TRUE FACE OF A GOD

Гэта казка іншага сям'і.

Сапраўдны твар Бога

A single god and his follower were sauntering down a path in the morning fog. He was an attractive, handsome god with golden-blond hair. His follower was a young elven girl with long raven-black hair and scarlet eyes. The god was holding several bouquets. The bunches of large white flowers were trembling.

There was a figure waiting for them up ahead.

"…Loki?" Dionysus murmured.

"Yo," Loki responded, raising a hand. Lefiya was standing beside her as a guard.

"Come here often?" Loki asked, watching the god from behind as he bent over to set the flowers down.

Accompanied by Loki, Dionysus and Filvis had come to the city's southeast quarter's First Graveyard—better known as the Adventurers Graveyard. It was a cemetery set aside for adventurers who had lost their lives. Rows upon rows of white headstones lined the ground. That early in the morning, there was not a soul around, save the four of them. It was serene.

"Yes…From time to time, I come here so I don't forget this feeling."

Dionysus stood up from where he sat with several headstones in front of him, markers indicating the resting place of the remains of none other than his own followers.

They had been lost more than four months ago, likely because they had happened to witness something related to the vividly colored monsters. He had joined forces with Loki to avenge them.

"…"

As a goddess, Loki knew that leaving a tribute to them had no meaning. Those children's souls had already returned to the heavens. A lump of withered flesh was all that was left buried beneath the headstones. There was no one there whose regrets needed to be soothed. No one there to be repaid. All Dionysus was doing was emulating the custom of the residents of the mortal realm.

But she did not think that the act itself was entirely without meaning, either. Because Loki had lost some of her beloved children in Knossos, too.

"What did you say?"

"An apology. Nothing else."

The only feelings the gods who stayed aboveground could express to their children were those of apology. Loki started to emulate him but stopped herself. She decided that she would not do something sentimental until she had weeded out all the evil that had robbed her of Leene and the rest. Lefiya lowered her eyes in the goddess's stead, and Filvis closed her eyes to avoid showing her feelings.

"Loki, I said it before. As far as I'm concerned, every god and goddess in this city is a suspect. Any one of them might be my children's enemy," Dionysus said as he kept staring at the graves.

"...Yeah."

"I will have their vengeance. I'm going to make sure that retribution finds the deity who devised all of this," he declared with his eyes fixed on the graves, as though announcing a vow he had sworn in his heart.

"Loki, shall I take a stab at what's on your mind? You think my familia would be a hindrance. You have no intention of letting us participate in the plan to attack in the near future."

"..."

"But I'm going to go out on a limb and ask: Let us participate in your plan." Slowly turning around, Dionysus's eyes locked straight onto Loki's.

She widened her eyes as she met his gaze.

"I heard what Ouranos is doing on his side. That the secret they were hiding had nothing to do with the truth that I'm after. In the end, I was just a fool stirring up trouble. I know you've no reason to trust me...However, even still, I would like you to bring me along."

His words resembled an entreaty, a supplication. Dionysus was always hiding behind a sweet mask, evasive in his speech to never reveal his true feelings. To have him unveil a strong will was a big deal. He did not raise his voice at all, but each and every word was packed with force.

"This isn't just about defeating the remnants of the Evils and that corrupted spirit. We must unmask the one going by the name Enyo."

"...True. As long as we don't crush the root of everything, this will just keep happening again."

"Exactly. And a god is required to pass judgment on a god...That's far too heavy a burden to have a child carry."

"..."

He left it unspoken, but what Dionysus was saying was that he was going to join the attack. It was the ultimate taboo for a mortal to "kill" a god—a mortal sin. If Enyo turned out to actually be a deity of some sort, then it was entirely possible that they would be able to get away if Loki's followers hesitated in the face of such a task. Because of that, they would need gods to accompany them.

Lefiya and Filvis looked up in shock at his request. There was a determined look on his face.

"Until all masterminds are uncovered and destroyed, I won't be able to complete my objective...Please, Loki. I beg of you."

A ray of morning sun started to shine on the corner of the grave-yard, beneath the shade of the towering city walls. Loki stared into his glass-colored eyes for a while as he made no attempt to look away. After a few seconds, she opened her mouth.

"...I understand."

Leaving the Adventurers Graveyard, they returned to the town. The four of them walked through the neighborhood as people started to bustle around, signaling the start of a new day.

"When will it begin?"

"We haven't decided on a specific day. But be ready to go at a moment's notice. This time, we're not just borrowing Fil-Fil. We're going to need the help of all of *Dionysus Familia*."

"Understood. We'll start preparing immediately. If you don't mind, I'm going to let my whole familia know the details. That okay?"

The two gods discussed the plan as they walked.

Behind them, Lefiya's elongated ears twitched listening to their conversation. "Huh?" Her head tilted a bit in confusion. Noticing that Filvis, who was walking beside her, looked disheartened that Loki had settled on an uncouth nickname—"Fil-Fil"—she rushed to comfort her.

"Look! It's Lord Dionysus!"

"It really is! What a nice way to start the day!"

All of a sudden, a pair of demi-human girls walking past called out, mainly to Dionysus.

"A date this early in the morning? And with three different girls!"

"Or are you coming back after a night out? How naughty!"

"W-wait a minute! Wait just a minute there, cuties! Don't go countin' me in this dumbass's harem!"

"Ha-ha-ha, it would be nice if that was the case, but unfortunately, I don't have that kind of relationship with them. And besides, one of them is a rather unfeminine goddess who's difficult to handle."

"I'll tear your leg off and shove it up your—!"

As Loki half groaned and half shouted, Dionysus stopped and flashed the pair a sweet smile. The girls shrieked excitedly, and after they had their share of squeals, they reluctantly continued heading to work. Lefiya was bewildered but let out a short, muffled scream as she noticed Filvis glaring daggers at her patron god's back. Dionysus displayed a will of iron, ignoring the looks from his follower as he waved back to the girls.

"Hey! What just happened?"

"What do you mean? Some acquaintances. I've often gone to buy flowers at the store at which they work."

"Oh, piss off..."

"It's inevitable, Loki. I am a god, after all. And I'm just a little bit more gentlemanly than the other goofy gods, which means I end up looking attractive to them. That's all it is."

"Screw you, acting like hot shit! You sleazeball!"

"What's with the correction? 'Hot shit' wasn't harsh enough for you, Loki?"

Loki started cursing him with a straight face as he elegantly ran his hand through his hair.

However, that was not the end of it. The residents who passed by spoke to Dionysus. If it had just been women, Loki would have called him out, saying, *You poseur, quit mistaking shadiness for mysteriousness!* but—

"Oh, Lord Dionysus! It's been a while!"

"It sure has, Gondo. I see you're hard at work, even this early."

"Thanks to you! Oh, that reminds me. Why don't you try a glass! I was experimenting with a method of making it in a larger vat like they do in the country of Gizia, and the results were fantastic!"

"Oh really? Well now, I'll have to try some, then!"

"Lord Dionysus! Make sure you come by my store, too!"

—Dionysus was popular with men, too. Particularly humans and dwarves with deep voices and thick bodies. Loki was taken aback, stopping in her tracks, confusion steeped on her face.

"…I'm surprised. Lord Dionysus is popular…"

"Popular, huh…? I mean, it's all just acquaintances he's made through wine, though…"

As Lefiya blinked in shock, Filvis sighed with a blank look on her face. Before them, Dionysus's eyes twinkled as he held a glass of wine, letting it play across his palate. He gushed over the wine, and his excitement was more palpable than when he spoke with the girls. His joy was almost childish. Surprised by this side of Dionysus that went beyond her expectations, Lefiya stifled a little giggle.

"What's this? Lord Dionysus is coming by?"

"Hey, Jenna. How are Sue and Holly? Aren't they almost five now?"

"What…? You remembered?!"

"I would never forget a winemaker who makes delicious wine, nor his family."

"You're too kind! Sue, Holly, come here!"

"Ah! Lord Dionysus!"

"Hey! Hey! Let us join your familia!"

They were on a shopping street lined with stone buildings and tiled with cobblestones hosting a wide array of shops. Many of them were apparently run with the help of their owners' families. It was an idyllic image of a working-class neighborhood, with children running around, playing in the streets, and adults occasionally scolding them good-naturedly.

And on that street, warm voices kept calling Dionysus's name—from those young and old, men and women of all races. It was clear everyone loved Dionysus. With her mind blown, Loki moved beside the god who had finally broken free of the winemaker's family.

"...I honestly never would have pegged you for this."

"That I'd have this kind of a relationship with children, you mean? As the patron god of a more medium-sized familia, I try to stay active in the area." Dionysus shrugged. "And besides...this is one of the charms of the mortal realm, right?"

Respect was evident in the second half of his response. His eyes sharpened, observing the lively shopping street.

"This is a blessing, what we see before our eyes. But there are people who wish to destroy this happiness, who are trying to incite an *orgia*."

Another word from the language of the gods.

"*Orgia*...A feast of madness, huh?"

If the lid on the Dungeon, Babel, was destroyed, and Orario along with it, monsters would begin to disperse aboveground again—just like in the ancient times when everything was overrun. If that happened, it certainly would be a frenzied *orgia*: Men would become pitiful sacrifices to the monsters as women and children desperately fled in tears, attacked from behind by claws and fangs.

The cries of pandemonium would be interspersed with blood as reason and order disappeared from the mortal realm.

Dionysus watched over the scene before his eyes with a sort of righteous indignation.

"...Well, that aside, I can't say it's easy to stomach you being so popular around town. Who were those cute little girls? They looked like they had bright futures ahead of them! 'I want to join your familia when I get older!' The only thing nicer than that would have been, 'I want to marry you when I get older!'" Loki tried to poke some fun at him.

"Not to be rude to them, but I'm the one who decides who joins my familia…especially given the current situation."

Dionysus's reaction was heartless, a complete reversal of the smile he'd shown those children earlier. He was entirely pragmatic.

Loki did not think it was unfeeling, though. Being duplicitous and hiding behind appearances weren't actions limited to gods. In fact, it was far more godlike to engage in this behavior. It would be more suspicious to have gods who were always smiling, filled with love, and never harboring any hidden intentions.

"Gaaaack! I'm gonna be late for my job?!"

…Well, there were always exceptions.

"Noisy as ever, aren'tcha…Itty-Bitty?"

"Gah…Loki?! Running into you at this wee hour…W-were you waiting here to laugh at me for being late?!"

"Who has the time for that kind of crap?"

"This was supposed to be my first day helping out at the sisters' shop! Of all things, coming to laugh at me here…? You demon! You loafer!"

"Don't go explaining things I don't wanna hear! Like I care!"

Wearing the uniform of the Jyaga Maru Kun stand, the goddess Hestia was filled with love. She did not have a secretive bone in her body. Though whether it was a smile or rage on her face as she called Loki out was debatable.

"Hmph! Really? Aren't you the incarnation of an idler just drink-ing the day away?!"

"I can't really deny the main point, but I don't want to hear it from you, dumbass! I've been super busy lately! Getting wrapped up in a battle for the fate of the city, crazy busy day and night!"

"What a load! If you're going to lie, pick a more believable one, idiot!"

"You've done it now, you damn cow!!!"

Responding tit for tat, the two of them started to scuffle as if it was just the natural order of things. Loki was taking advantage of her height and pulling on both of Hestia's cheeks—"Take that!"—while Hestia was trying to resist her, but in standard Hestia fashion, she could only let out a muffled screech as her cheeks were stretched and kneaded like dough. Lefiya desperately tried to stop them, but the goddesses' quarrel did not stop. Filvis seemed exasperated by this display.

With a surprised look on his face, Dionysus smiled and bowed to Hestia.

"What a surprise to meet you here. Are you well, Hestia?"

"Ah! Dionysus! Long time no see!"

Because of her hostility toward Loki, she had not noticed anything else until she pressed on her swollen cheeks and finally saw Dionysus. Meanwhile, Loki and Lefiya were both surprised to see Dionysus of all people bow respectfully and nobly to Hestia.

"Hey! Dionysus…What sort of relationship do you have with this shrimp?"

"What? Our territories happened to be close in heaven. You could call it a neighborly relationship."

"Oh yeah…She's from the same place as you, right?"

"Yes, here stands the glory of Olympus."

Hermes was from the same homeland as Dionysus, too, as were Hephaistos, Demeter, and Ikelos, who had been cast out from the city the other day. And most famously, Zeus and Hera. It irritated Loki just remembering them.

Thinking back, there certainly were quite a few gods and goddesses from Olympus residing in Orario.

"Seriously?! Dionysus, you're hanging out with Loki?! You should be more careful who you play with! Seriously! Like, really, really seriously!"

"You rotten shrimp…" Loki trembled as she raised her fist at the little goddess overreacting in her protests.

As the pair looked ready to start another scuffle, Dionysus laughed wryly and explained in order to smooth things over.

"Hestia is a wonderful goddess. I'm one of many who have been honored to receive her affection. Words of gratitude cannot begin to repay the debt I owe her from back when we were in the heavens," Dionysus explained in all honesty.

Loki's face drooped, as if the muscles in her cheeks were suddenly obliterated. In truth, it was a rather ugly look, the sort that a goddess should never show, even by mistake. Meanwhile, Hestia put her hands on her hips and thrust her chest out with pride.

"At the time, our territory had a rule to select the Twelve Gods...our representatives. I despaired at not being able to take part, but...then Hestia lent me a hand."

In the heavens where gods resided, there were territories similar to the countries of the mortal realm. And those territories had their own rules. Apparently, in their area, being one of the Twelve Gods represented an important position without any comparable substitute. And Hestia had relinquished it without a second thought, giving it to Dionysus.

"Yep! I let him trade places with me!"

"You probably just wanted to hole up in your temple and relax all day."

"D-don't be stupid!"

Turning away from Loki, who had hit the bull's-eye, Hestia seemed deeply moved as she looked up at Dionysus.

"Back then, he was always on edge. At any point, I could expect him to shout, 'The latent evil aura in my right fist will obliterate you assholes!' Yeah, it was super painful to watch."

"Could I ask you not to say things that will ruin my reputation? ...Really. I mean it..." Closing his eyes, Dionysus chuckled slightly as he ran his hand through his hair—but said hand was trembling.

What the hell happened between them?

""Lord Dionysuuuuuus! Come here!"" some of the children called out eagerly.

"Oh my...Excuse me," Dionysus said to the two goddesses before happily heading over toward the kids without a twinge of sorrow. In order to fulfill her job as his guard, Filvis went with him.

"...Huh, seems Dionysus is respected."

"Yeah. There should be a limit to surprise."

In contrast to Loki shrugging, Hestia looked intently at the god.

"It seems like Dionysus has gotten over his 'illness.'"

That's what she said.

"...Illness?"

In that instant, Loki creaked to a halt before slowly rotating her head toward Hestia, who was neither scowling nor smiling. There were no signs that Hestia was pulling her leg as she watched over the god.

"...What do you mean by that, shrimp? What are you talking about?"

Hestia turned back around at the question. The smaller goddess arched her brow dubiously as she met Loki's gaze. "Aren't you hanging out with him because you're one and the same, Loki?"

"The same...? *Me*? Similar to *him*?"

"I thought you made an odd combo at first, but that would explain it."

"Hey! Wait just one minute. What are you actually trying to say?"

At that moment, Loki realized that she was perplexed, noticing a strange uneasiness rising up in her chest.

What are you talking about? That Dionysus and I are the same? That we have things in common? The part where we both manipulate people? That we both like to drink? What are you trying to say, Hestia? She struggled and stammered as she tried to put it all together, questioning the goddess in front of her.

"You both seriously got into it with other gods."

"!!"

"That's why I said you're similar. You got into some serious knock-down, drag-out fights with other gods, too. Didn't you, Loki?" Hestia looked at her with a piercing glare.

. But Loki was not in a state of mind to be bothered by her pointed gaze. Sure, she'd gotten into a handful of murderous scuffles with other gods and goddesses in the heavens. In fact, she'd been so brutal and unprecedentedly destructive that those who knew her only once she'd mellowed out after coming down to the mortal realm and getting a familia could not begin to picture it. She had been so troublesome that she'd earned herself the stupid nickname "the ultimate trickster in all the heavens."

Loki was amazed. She had never heard anything like that about Dionysus before, which was also the case for Lefiya, who was listening beside her.

"…Do you remember any of the people involved?"

"I guess I'd say everyone? Back then, Dionysus had a really bad temper, and he'd blow up at anyone who happened to be around. It's like his usual serene disposition is a complete facade."

"…"

"Buuut if I had to name a certain person, then it'd probably be Zeus…and outside the Twelve Gods, maybe Ouranos?" Hestia continued without taking notice of Loki's silence as she tapped her slender finger on her chin.

Ouranos again, huh…?

Dionysus had been suspicious of the Guild even before they'd started working together. Or more to the point, he had been suspicious of Ouranos, who stood behind the scenes of the Guild. Until the situation with the Xenos came to light, he had been adamant in his distrust.

What happened between the two of them up there to make him that mad at the old man?

"Why was Dionysus picking a fight with Ouranos?"

"That's why I said it's an illness. Though maybe calling it a spasm would be better. I told you Dionysus was touchy way back, didn't I?"

"…"

"When he got into it with Ouranos and the others, it was always over small things. Dionysus was constantly harping on them one-sidedly. Well, if you want to know exactly what triggered his fits and outbursts, you'd probably have to ask the actual people involved.

"It's not like I know their personal relations," Hestia added casually. At the same time, the little goddess who was the protector of those who prayed for aid looked a little bit sad, as if she was remembering the precarious situation.

In reality, there was a significant number of gods and goddesses who had festered in boredom up in the heavens, which cleared up when they came down to the mortal realm. Loki was one of them herself. However, Dionysus had not given off even the slightest hint that he was, too, in all the time she had dealt with him. In fact, she was struggling to imagine it.

"…What did you feel when you saw Dionysus back then?" Loki switched subjects.

How had he seemed at the time to someone from the same homeland? To someone who had seen him up close?

"Hmm…I thought he was scary, I think."

And again, Loki was blown away—to hear Hestia say he was scary.

That slacker was popular in her own weird way: The most famous one from her network is Hephaistos, known for being stubborn up there. And Penia, too. And even that crazy, psycho, hyper-ultra-hysterical Hera. There were lots of gods and goddesses who made fun of her for being a kiddie goddess, too, but she has some weird connections with a ton of people.

For better or for worse, Hestia was fair: She didn't discriminate or set people apart from one another. Though she got plenty mad at Loki, who picked fights with her or made fun of her, she held real authority, too. Loki suspected Ouranos and even Zeus acknowledged her. She was plain, but her status as a goddess, the one who ruled over the immortal flame, was undeniably high.

And for that Hestia to say Dionysus was scary…

"That's why when they started brawling over the seat among the Twelve Gods, I said I'd step down if they were really gonna fight. I don't like to be in tense situations."

At the time, Hestia had hopped down from her chair, chirping, "Be sure to play nice!" before booking it out of the temple of the Twelve Gods. Loki could totally imagine it happening, which made her weak. But because Hestia had given up her seat, Dionysus's illness had not developed into anything serious.

"Well, no one else seemed to notice it. Maybe I was imagining things," Hestia concluded, looking up and glancing forward. She saw Dionysus surrounded by a ring of children wearing smiles. "But if this is the situation, then I guess there's nothing to worry about now. That's good."

Standing next to her, Loki did not respond, about to press Hestia for more information.

"Hey, Itty-Bitty, tell me more—"

"Wait! Look at the time! I'm going to be late for my part-time job!" Hestia shrieked and dashed away, suddenly remembering her current predicament.

"Saying what you want and running away..."

Without enough time to stop her, Loki gradually lowered her outstretched hand as Hestia's small form trailed away. Left behind, Loki looked back at Dionysus, as did Lefiya, who was flustered. The aristocratic god seemed composed and almost loving as he played with the children.

The sun was just beginning to lean toward the west around noon.

The main street in the city was jam-packed with people. It seemed there were more throngs of demi-humans of all kinds coming and going than usual. As if to prove the point, people from the slum grouped together to finish shopping for the minimal supplies they could afford.

The scene of Daedalus Street becoming a battlefield with the appearance of armed monsters was still fresh in their minds. While the Guild, *Ganesha Familia*, and *Loki Familia* were continuing the reconstruction work, the residents of the Labyrinth District had been given temporary housing elsewhere until repairs were finished. They had been evicted from the slums and carried on with their lives on the main streets.

That said, it wasn't as though the residents of Daedalus Street, much less the people ambling around its road, had faces cast with bitter or sad expressions. They were relieved that the threat of monsters aboveground had disappeared, restoring some semblance of peace in their lives.

Yes, everyone was enjoying peace. No one had noticed the true menace, the countdown to the city's destruction, that was slowly ticking.

"To think Lord Dionysus was so unstable when he was in the heavens..." Lefiya whispered, glancing out at the street filled with smiles but not really processing any of them.

Beneath a large magic-stone streetlight, the fragmentary thought passed her lips and melted into the background noise. Recalling Hestia's comments, she started to wonder, *Does Miss Filvis know about that story...?*

"Sorry, Lefiya. Did I keep you waiting?"

"Ah...Miss Filvis!"

The elf in question weaved her way through the crowd before appearing in front of Lefiya.

"...? What? Something happen?"

"Ah! No, it's nothing." Lefiya flashed her a bitter smile, instead of offering a proper explanation, as the incident with Dionysus crossed her mind.

She suspected that would be a taboo topic to approach with Filvis, a devotee, and knew that a noble elf would still keep supporting her patron god—regardless of his sordid past.

"I'm so sorry for asking for time out of your busy schedule..."

"No, I wanted to talk with you, too. Before the start of the Knossos operation," Filvis added in a lowered voice.

They started to move away from the lamppost where they had met up. After their gods had dismissed their meeting and Loki had returned to the manor, Lefiya had been relieved of her duty as guard. She had been waiting until now for Filvis to finish getting Dionysus back to their home.

Though she'd been the one to invite Filvis, Lefiya didn't have any reason in particular to ask her out. But things had been so hectic lately that they hadn't had many opportunities to talk. What she really wanted was to have an unhurried conversation with Filvis for the first time in a while.

She suggested going to some café, but Filvis shook her head and took Lefiya along with her instead, slipping out of the streets and reaching a high point where they could overlook the cityscape. With no one around, there was no concern that someone might overhear their conversation.

"It seems it was just decided that the other familia members… that the entirety of *Dionysus Familia* will be taking part in the operation."

"Is that…so?…I suppose that would be the case." Lefiya nodded deeply as Filvis gazed out over the city.

This time, the operation was going to need manpower. Even though their combat capabilities did not begin to compare to *Loki Familia*'s, it was inevitable that *Dionysus Familia* would take part, based on numbers alone. It would not just be Filvis by herself as it had been in the past. Dionysus was serious about this, too.

"Lefiya…are you going to join this operation?"

"…? Yes, of course."

Filvis had her back to her fellow elf as Lefiya furrowed her brow.

She was feeling a keen sense of déjà vu. Almost four months ago, she had been asked the same thing when she was doing her special training before the expedition. That was when Filvis had taught her Dio Grail. And now—

"—Lefiya, won't you leave Orario?" she suggested.

"Wha…?"

"Until this operation is over, go someplace outside the city—some far-off town, or even an elven village would be fine. If you don't want to go alone, then I'll join you. I'd rather not remove myself from protecting Lord Dionysus, but I can leave it to the others, including Aura, who are taking part in the operation. And it shouldn't be a very serious blow to *Loki Familia* if you're missing—"

"W-wait! Please wait a minute, Miss Filvis!" Lefiya had raised her voice to a ragged shout without realizing it.

She leaned forward toward Filvis, who had been speaking without facing her the whole time.

"Why are you saying this out of nowhere?! I might not have that much value to contribute, but I could never cowardly run away before the decisive battle! I'm an elf, a noble race, after all!" she yammered on, confused by the sudden proposal and beginning to question Filvis's real motives.

Filvis fell silent. After a short pause, she turned around.

"You…are going to die."

"What…?"

"The most recent attack made that perfectly clear." With a critical, pointed gaze, she looked at Lefiya in total seriousness.

"Wh-what?" she stammered, sweat beading on her brow. Filvis's comment started to ring like a bell.

During her first expedition to Knossos, Lefiya had been exceedingly rash. In fact, she'd been so careless that Filvis, who had gone with her, had scolded her loudly. And after that, she had encountered Thanatos, the patron god of the enemy; found herself surrounded; and then faced off against Gugalanna, a bull-type demi-spirit. To put it bluntly, it would not have been at all strange for her to have been killed. Filvis was holding a grudge over what had happened then. Or perhaps she was nervous about what it portended.

"You neglect your needs and are keen on sacrificing yourself."

"Th-that's not—"

"No, I know. You'll definitely…end up falling into despair," Filvis revealed, stating her true feelings.

Lefiya could hear an undertone of pleading, of desperation, in her voice.

"For the first time since that day…I was scared of losing something. I'd thought I would only ever have an attachment to Lord Dionysus…but I'm terrified…of losing you."

Lefiya understood "that day" to mean the Twenty-Seventh-Floor Nightmare.

Filvis had been scorned with the taboo name of Banshee, which had frozen over her heart. Had she really become so attached to her?

"Please, Lefiya…Could you listen to my wish?"

It made Lefiya unimaginably happy—indescribably joyous. Facing Filvis's earnest gaze, she looked down for a second.

But she raised her head with an unshakable resolve.

"I'm sorry, Miss Filvis."

"..."

"I will not run away."

Filvis's scarlet eyes narrowed in sadness. Feeling her heart ache, Lefiya forcefully opened her own eyes.

"Besides...that human managed to become a Level Four!"

"Huh...?"

"Bell Cranell! Bell Cranell!! He got a new title, confirmed for an expedition mission! They're even saying laughable things about him—like how he's the adventurers' rising star! But he's no such thing! He's more...more...! You've heard the rumors, right?!"

"Ah, yes..."

"I'm not angry about it, obviously! If I asked Loki, I'm sure I could rank up to Level Four, too! It's not like I've been surpassed by him! Though he did catch up to me...! B-but the real fight starts now!"

"L-Lefiya...?"

"Yes! That's why I can't run away! That human didn't run away, even faced with that black minotaur! It was so heated, so intense, so sublime that it was like a fire burning inside me! E-even I could do that...! Or are you saying you don't think I can accomplish the same feat as that human?!"

"I—I didn't say that."

"If I try! I can do it! I'll show you!" she howled, squeezing her eyes shut, clenching her fists as her face turned bright red.

Partway through, her anger or regret or something flared up within her, and there was no stopping her. But those were her honest thoughts.

Filvis watched her fellow elf seething with indignation as she renewed her resolve. As the one who had made the request in the first place, she started to break out in a cold sweat.

"...That's why." Finally, Lefiya's heated emotions cooled down as she met Filvis's scarlet eyes. "I will support the others, like Miss Aiz. I will face fear and despair...and I will save them."

That was her pride as a magic user. She wanted to become the sword and shield to save the adventurers who protected her. What Riveria and Aiz had taught her became Lefiya's vow.

She refused Filvis's desire. The shy mage was nowhere to be found anymore. Just like a certain boy, the girl had grown strong.

A breeze passed by them, causing one's silken, raven-colored hair and one's golden-yellow locks to ripple and wave. Time passed atop the high point far from the bustle of the city. After a little while, Filvis smiled.

"You're seriously a selfish, stubborn...noble elf."

"Ah..."

It was as if she had already known what Lefiya's response would be. It was pure and, at the same time, empty.

"Then I will protect you. I won't let you die—even if it's only you."

"Miss Filvis..."

"Even at the cost of my own life."

It was an exchange like one they'd had before. As Lefiya had come to her own conclusion, Filvis had made a vow. Lefiya was about to add that she would rather Filvis not say something with an ominous tone, but she stopped herself. She recognized in those scarlet eyes a determination that would not back down. Just like her own.

Which was why Lefiya relaxed her face and smiled.

"Let's win. In this battle. And come back together...the two of us."

"...Yes. Let's do our best to make it happen," Filvis replied in her usual manner, causing them to exchange smiles.

Beneath the blue sky, they started to walk away. Leaving behind the place where they had expressed their resolves, they moved forward.

"But...going outside the city. That might be nice."

"What?"

Walking together, Lefiya had suddenly spoken. She smiled at Filvis, who seemed surprised by her comment.

"We've been fighting ever since I first got to know you. After this fight is over, why don't we go on a trip? Just the two of us?"

"Lefiya...".

"If we're going all out, how about a visit to my home village?

Before long, the Great Tree will have its crown of light. Apparently, it's unique to Wishe Forest, and you won't be able to see it in any other village. It's so beautiful! It's like it has a crown of flowers with glittering specks of light scattered all around it..."

"...Like the cherry blossoms? In the Far East?"

"Yes! And there's even a flower garden that only I know about! It's unbelievably pretty! Let's go there together."

She was talking about her home, Wishe Forest.

It would be no less than wonderful to see Lefiya's treasured sights together. Even if someone had found her secret garden, it wouldn't be any less lovely. And the memories they were to make there would be theirs—and theirs alone.

Let's make it through this battle and go see it. That was what Lefiya was offering.

"Yes..."

As Lefiya beamed, Filvis wore a pure smile.

"Once this is all done, we'll go. I promise."

In *Freya Familia*'s home, Folkvangr, familia members battled intensely day and night.

It wouldn't be right to call it a mock battle—but rather training by way of death matches. In order to win their patron goddess's favor, they crossed swords with intense force, desperate to become stronger than the next person.

—But on that day, the members of *Freya Familia* stopped moving. Inside the walled-in field, armed and standing still, they all faced one direction, united.

It was dusk. The sky was turning red in the west. They had their attention stolen by the battle unfolding before them.

"Argh!"

"Wha—?!"

A thunderous roar resounded, kicking up chunks of dirt. As clods of earth and plants rained down, the body of the blond-haired, golden-eyed girl soared through the air, blown away by the impact. Aiz had managed to dodge the slash the boaz man had unleashed from high above his head by a razor-thin margin, but there was no time to shudder at the strike that shattered the ground because she was forced to deal with an instantaneous follow-up attack closing in from the side.

"Hah!"

Her trusted Desperate knocked away the large sword approaching her. As Ottar narrowed his eyes, Aiz accelerated with a bravery that left the onlooking *Freya Familia* members breathless. They crossed swords again, and again, and again.

It was yet another day of training with Ottar—another day of practice with the city's strongest, the Level 7, that she had requested and that unleashed a cacophony of sounds.

Ottar gave her no advice. He simply exchanged blows with her, and that was all.

It was a harsh, real combat style of training. As if he was telling her with their crossed blades to learn through the course of fighting with him. She'd given Bell the same treatment, since she was not very good at expressing herself with words, but it made what she did to Bell seem cute in comparison—because Ottar had no intention of guiding her.

As if considering it obvious that Aiz would have to forge her own route, the boaz warrior hit her with his overwhelming strength. He was not using a sword with a dulled blade or anything. If she was not careful, she could easily die. And if Aiz made a stupid mistake, Ottar would probably mercilessly cut her in half.

Aiz was battered, day after day. The special training began before the sun rose, and they kept fighting until after the sun set. The only time she could lay on the ground and look up at the sky was right around when the day was about to bleed into tomorrow. Once all was done, she collapsed on the ground and passed out for a brief moment before beginning the training again early in the morning. She was not even given a bed. The girl named Helen, who was attending to Freya, had refused to let it pass and given her a change

of clothes and a damp cloth to wash herself with, but if not for her, Aiz would not even have bathed.

It was the seventh day of her special training. Aiz realized she was in the same position as the white-haired boy had been before. In any normal circumstance, she might have chuckled, been tickled, found it funny, but she did not have any capacity left for that. The sword in her right hand constantly flickered, parrying the never-ending storm of blows raining down on her.

"Slow."

"—Gh?!"

She was struck by a powerful blow. Unable to fully block it, Aiz was sent rolling across the ground before she finally stopped herself, kneeling on one knee.

While Aiz breathed heavily, Ottar looked totally unruffled, not sweating at all.

Aiz's wind had already run out from casting Airiel at the start of the training session, but before noon, she was out of Mind, and the combat turned into a pure hand-to-hand fight. She continued to cover the massive physical burden of strong magic with the elixirs that Ottar forced her to take.

What was most amazing was Ottar's bottomless tenacity. Regardless of whether she used her wind or not, he had the overwhelming strength to totally shut her down. With frustration showing on her face, she roughly wiped away the mud covering her scratched cheeks.

"…Sword Princess."

"…?"

Ottar abandoned his stance and, for the first time during their training, asked her a question: "How strong is the opponent you have to fight for you to go this far?"

Ottar was acknowledging Aiz's resolve and intensity to endure the days of training as she came at him as though a desperate, cornered animal. For the first time, the city's strongest showed an interest in the goal that had driven her to seek out special training with him.

"…I don't know. I can't see a cap to my enemy," Aiz responded with her honest impression.

The creature with bloodred hair flashed through her mind. When Aiz thought she had surpassed her by leveling up to Level 6, Levis had become an enhanced species that leapfrogged past Aiz again at an inhuman speed. If Levis was increasing her strength by gathering magic stones, there was no longer any way to do a simple calculation of her strength. After struggling to put it into words, Aiz finally shared her perspective.

"But in pure Status terms…she's definitely stronger than you as you're facing me right now."

"…"

While Aiz thought back to Levis's strength when they had clashed in Knossos, Ottar's eyes narrowed. As if she had fanned the flames of his fighting spirit.

One of the most frightening things about the boaz was that he wasn't fighting at full strength—no use of magic or even any skills. Ottar was simply facing her with only his pure ability. And he was overpowering her with just his physical prowess despite her wind and other deadly techniques. He made free use of his unimaginable battle experience and an overwhelming depth of tactics. More than anything, considering Ottar's race, she was sure that he still had an ace up his sleeve.

"A creature, huh? I heard about it from Tammuz, but…"

Aiz was shocked to hear him say the word *creature* out of nowhere, but Ottar paid her no heed as he continued.

"Sword Princess. After exchanging blows with you, I've understood something."

"?"

"You are not as skilled as you think in combat against other people."

"?!"

Aiz was so startled at his sudden declaration that her shock was almost audible. She was not full of herself by any means, but she did have some pride in having worked hard to get where she was—plus some shred of self-confidence in her nickname as the Sword

Princess. To have that negated by someone who stood above her, by the undisputed strongest man in the city, was a blow to her self-esteem.

"Compared to those in your generation, you're certainly excellent, plenty strong…But compared to Finn or me, you're missing something."

"…!"

"Our generation had Zeus and Hera, monsters that acted as if our counterattacks were nothing…During that time, the young people in Orario had no choice but to steep themselves in battle against other people."

The words of the warrior who slid into memories of days past struck home with Aiz. It was the turbulent era that Finn and the others had managed to survive, the city's Dark Ages—the cruel era that had continued until the end of the struggle with the Evils.

Was there no way to overcome the difference in experience? Was there no way for her to win against Levis as an adventurer? Aiz chewed on her lip.

"But don't get it twisted. That's not where your real ability lies."

Right then, Ottar's tone changed.

"Your sword's true nature does not lie in fighting people—it's a weapon for slaughtering monsters."

"!!" Aiz was blown away.

When she snapped her head up, she saw that the green eyes looking down at her were the same as always.

"I've seen you fight in the Dungeon many times. And after this training, I'm sure of it. Your sword's sole purpose is killing monsters… It takes it to the logical extreme, removing all extraneous concerns, without concern for wounds. An obsession. In that regard, you've surpassed me—and the rest as well, including Finn."

Sword techniques wielded for the sole purpose of killing monsters. A murderous blade for slaughtering countless monsters, creating a mountain of their corpses. Ottar was saying that in that regard alone, she had left them in the dust. Aiz gazed in wonder and agitation as she foresaw what he was about to say.

"When you fought this creature, were you perceiving it as a person?"

"—...!"

That was correct. Aiz had crossed blades with Levis as if she were an adventurer or a warrior, just like Aiz was. That was entirely because she had a human form, because a mutual understanding had been possible. After she knew that Levis was a creature, she had stood against her as a warrior.

"Once you perceive an enemy as a person, even if it's a monster, you have no chance of winning."

The sword in her hands trembled at his assertion. There was no way he could know Aiz's ability. And yet, it was as if he knew the full story of the skill engraved on her back.

It was true, if she wielded that power while fighting against Levis, the fight would go differently than it had in the past. But the source of her strength—her obsession—was wavering. Because of the resolve of the boy who she had fought under the moonlight and the tears of the dragon girl, it had lost its home. Faced with Aiz, who showed an even deeper anguish than before, Ottar's eyes sharpened.

"...You lost your way after confronting the armed monsters, huh?"

"!"

Just how much does this man—?

It was as if he could clearly see into her mind. Sweat rolling down her face, her throat dry, Aiz started to move her mouth before she realized it.

"Why do you know...?"

"I don't know anything about you. I don't know, but I *get* it. None other than your own sword shows just how half-hearted your resolve is."

The warrior was saying that the flying sparks and clashing blades had shown him everything. Aiz looked down at her hands. The silver blade reflected the face that was concealing her doubt.

"I can't share an answer or any method to resolve your conflict. And I've no interest in making that happen. However, if I was to say something, then—" The city's strongest adventurer halted. "Why do you think you can beat an enemy more powerful than you without pouring everything you have into it?"

Aiz was shaken even harder by this comment than everything leading up to it. She was unsure. In truth, she was trying to put off a resolution to her doubts. Given the existence of the Xenos, should she regard monsters as absolute evil that must be destroyed—or not? But the warrior standing before her shrugged off that concern. He was telling her that if there was a wall that she needed to overcome, then she should overcome it with all her might.

In the next moment, Ottar gave off a completely different vibe as he stepped sharply toward her. With her eyes wide open, Aiz managed to raise Desperate and catch his forceful blow.

"There is a flame in you. A black determination that will destroy you if you make a single misstep."

"…!"

"Do not let it swallow you up. Control it. And remember."

His mysterious statement triggered a shock. And he accompanied it with an unapologetic slash of his sword. The girl was visibly surprised as the boaz man beat that truth into her.

"The enemy you're going to face—is nothing more than a brief stop in the grand scheme of things."

"!!"

A scene flashed before Aiz's eyes. A wild winter background. A bawling little girl who had lost everything. And a single wish that she had to achieve.

"—Ghhhhh!"

Aiz howled. As she deflected Ottar's blade, the clash let out an explosive boom, and she lunged forward, beginning a raging counterattack. Her back ached with the sacred letters engraved in her skin.

But it was not the flames of destruction that consumed Aiz. Her eyes were fixed on the goal standing before her—fighting spirit focused on a single enemy.

Control it without being consumed. Don't mistake what it's for. Don't destroy because of hatred. It's all for the sake of winning—to protect my friends, my familia, and this city.

"Aaaaaaaaaaaaaaaahhhhhhhh!"

It sparked a fire in Aiz's resolve. With a strength that she had not wielded before, she kicked up a storm of steel.

"That's good—"

It was a breakthrough that could not have happened were it not for Ottar. The words he spoke would not have been able to reach her if they had come from Riveria or Gareth, Finn or Loki, or those who knew her past. It was something she could learn only from him, someone who had no connection to her, the man known as the Warlord. A means of resolution.

Aiz's sword accelerated as she focused on the enemy she had to defeat. The warrior standing before her overlapped with the image of that woman.

Narrowing his eyes, Ottar responded to those flames using only his strength.

CHAPTER 4

AVENGERS
~ Knossos ~
War

Гэта казка іншага сям'і.

Мсціўцы
~ Кноскі вайны ~

Aiz Wallenstein

LEVEL 6

Strength: H100 -> 154 Defense: H117 ->153
Dexterity: H131 ->19 Agility: H112 ->174 Magic: H154 -> G202
Hunter: G Immunity: G Knight: I Spirit Healing: I

"A total growth over two fifty...I dunno where you went, but that must have been one hell of a training session."

She could hear Loki stifling a laugh behind her. Without anything to cover her upper half, Aiz looked at the Status update sheet that the goddess handed her and quietly clenched her fist.

She held the sheet to a torch and burned it. Watching the red flame peter out, she donned her combat outfit and looked out the window.

"All right, with that, the arrangements are all set. Today will be the start of the war."

The day of the assault on Knossos. The sunrise was just starting to peek over the horizon in the east.

In the city's southeast corner, an oppressive air was settling in around Daedalus Street. Battle-ready adventurers and a heavily armed force of military police were milling around. The former were from *Ganesha Familia*, who worked to maintain the city's order. The latter were members of the Guild.

There were currently no residents of the slums anywhere to be seen. On the surface, that was because of rebuilding the neighborhood. Under the pretext of restoring Daedalus Street after the armed monsters had turned it into a battlefield, the residents had been moved to temporary housing to the city's northwest at the instruction of the Guild.

The truth was that they'd been displaced to keep them from getting dragged into the operation that was about to begin. That was the reason *Loki Familia* had worked together with the other factions to help the reconstruction effort after the Xenos had returned belowground: to set up camp in the Labyrinth District without raising questions or causing a panic, to have a natural excuse for why the residents were being evacuated, and to establish a tight net around Knossos. Those outlaws who refused to follow the orders to leave were all caught and forced out.

The more perceptive people had probably taken notice. While the daily hustle and bustle was beginning in the surrounding areas, Daedalus Street was unnaturally silent. There were no sounds emanating from it.

"Sister! How is this operation getting reported to the Guild members?!"

"You're yapping too loud, Ilta. They were told there might be a second entrance to the Dungeon, which is what they're investigating. Apparently, Royman pulled some strings to avoid any unnecessary confusion with the Guild's people."

In the central part of Daedalus Street, where *Ganesha Familia* had set up their base, a red-haired Amazon named Ilta was kicking up a fuss.

"Sorry...but it's super annoying! Why aren't we going to be part of the first strike or whatever they're calling it?! Gah! That tiny little prum, always bossing us around however he pleases!"

"Our mission is to ensure the defense of Daedalus Street. Obviously, we can't let normal people enter, but we've also gotta keep an eye out for people who might try to escape from inside. That's the point of roping them in," responded a tall woman with indigo hair. She was the leader of *Ganesha Familia*, Shakti Varma.

"And besides, it's not just us. *Hephaistos Familia* isn't going to be part of the first assault, either. Finn isn't underestimating us. Quite the opposite. He made the judgment to reserve forces for the battle to come."

"...Huh, now that you mention it, I haven't seen Cyclops around. The other smiths are one thing, but there's no way he wouldn't use her. You know anything about that, sister?"

"During the battle here, she apparently attacked *Loki Familia*. It's not like they don't trust her anymore, but for the sake of appearances, she was removed from this operation. She was worked up about it."

"What the hell was she thinking...?"

Ilta was exasperated by the predicament that Tsubaki Collbrande, the master smith and Level 5, had gotten herself into.

"...In the end, I really can't accept it. We lost Hashana in this mess, too, after all."

Ilta bit her lip, letting a complicated blend of emotions peek out on her face. Shakti was silent for a moment as she referred to getting revenge for Hashana, who had been brutally murdered in Rivira on the eighteenth floor.

"Don't be angry, Ilta! Stay cool! Yeah, just like me, Ganesha!"

"Shut it, Ganesha!"

"You're so annoying, Ganesha."

The god wearing an elephant mask made his appearance, striking a weird pose. Not shrinking back from his followers' curt responses, Ganesha straightened his spine and took on a different vibe.

"We don't have to be avengers. We'll continue to be the shield protecting the masses. Hashana would not have wanted us to lose our path because of him."

Shakti's and Ilta's eyes widened slightly in understanding. They nodded back in response to their patron god. Turning around, they looked toward the opening in a wall that led underground.

The entrance to the hidden demons' den.

The man-made labyrinth, Knossos.

"Hey, Amid! You're joining this operation, too?!" Tiona called out in surprise, which traveled down the stone passage, echoing.

While *Ganesha Familia* was on guard aboveground, *Loki Familia* and the other groups assigned to take part in the invasion were underground in a passage that connected to a door to Knossos. While adventurers were jostling around, Tiona and Tione went to meet the beautiful girl with long platinum hair.

"Yes, at the request of Captain Finn. Aaaand I wanted to take part myself. But before that…allow me to apologize for delaying the start of the operation because of our medicine production."

"Do you hear yourself? I mean, even the captain said if it wasn't for you guys preparing the anti-curse medicine, the success rate of this operation would plummet."

"Yeah! Yeah! 'Cause we wouldn't even be able to heal a single wound! That would make charging in a total *repeat!*"

"You mean total *defeat*, dumbass."

Amid cracked a teeny smile at the exchange between Tiona and Tione. This girl, known as the city's greatest healer, was not in her usual familia uniform or the normal battle clothes that she wore when going into the Dungeon with the sisters.

Instead, she donned white robes. They were reserved for instances when she was heading into a serious battle against the likes of a floor boss—and when she was going not as a normal healer but as Dea Saint. As the other *Loki Familia* members were captivated by the sight of the holy woman in her sacred garments, Tiona and Tione responded like always: "It's been a while since she's broken out that look" and "It feels weird because you're in a different outfit."

Amid smiled again, seeing her friends behaving as if nothing had changed.

"I take it you're coming with us, Amid?"

"Yes. I discussed with Captain Finn if I could join the northeast squad."

Nodding to Tiona, Amid looked out at the unit formed of people from several familias. The invasion force was not all gathered in one place by any means. They were divided up before the multiple doors to Knossos.

* * *

"Bete Loga!"

"Why. The. Hell. Are. You. Here. You Amazon brat?!"

In front of the southeast entrance to Knossos. As a few healers from *Dian Cecht Familia* were joining the group, Bete let out an angry roar directed at the young Amazon Lena Tully, who had appeared before him.

"I found out from Aisha! I was all like, hmm, I wonder what *Loki Familia* is up to!"

She was wearing particularly revealing clothes, showing plenty of her bronze skin without any reservations. Combined with her cutesy gestures, everything about her was over-the-top. The young Amazon wasn't fully mature yet.

She spoke excitedly, her eyes as wide as saucers. "I threw a big tantrum and said I'd tell everyone about all the stuff she was doing behind the scenes for *Hermes Familia* if she didn't let me know! And Aisha even said, 'Just do whatever you want!' Wow, love is an amazing thing!"

"Love?! You're just being a whiny, selfish brat!"

"Enough of that! Do you need me to resupply you with my love? I bet your body's all worked up waiting for the operation to start. Why don't you relax by embracing my youthful body?!"

Blam! His iron fist rained down immediately, crashing hard on her forehead. A thunderous *thud* rang out as his fist made contact with her skull as she continued to make no sense.

Lena fell backward and rolled around screaming "Ghnaaaaaaaaaargh?!" as she clutched her forehead with both hands.

The members of other familias who heard the conversation started to whisper, but they let out stifled squeals and averted their gazes when they saw Vanargand's bloodshot eyes glaring at them. The members of *Loki Familia* had become so numbed to their interactions that they paid it no mind. Their stance was that nothing bad would happen to them as long as they weren't directly involved in it.

Lena staggered to her feet as tears welled in her eyes, but she continued to smile, not discouraged in the least. "And plus, Aisha went

along with *Hestia Familia* on their expedition! And she told me to
not get involved in this at all!"

"Then don't do it, dumbass..."

"But it didn't feel right to stay behind!" Lena blabbed, refusing to
listen to him, which made Bete look genuinely stumped.

Lena leaned in. "Bete Loga! Let me come, too...!"

"Stop trying to go the extra mile when no one asked you to," Bete
responded, yanking on her head in an instant.

"Guohhh?!"

Bete was radiating murder. "You're not coming," he announced
with a serious face.

"Gh—..."

"You're in the minor leagues."

"..."

"Got it?"

"...Yes," Lena conceded meekly, nodding as she squashed her normal upbeat energy.

As a weak person, she understood exactly what he meant. She was
the one who had once caught Bete in a terrible predicament beneath
that gray sky that pelted rain, and Lena drew back miserably with
frustration and sadness etched across her face.

"...Stay with *Ganesha Familia* aboveground. Okay?"

With that, he turned his back on her, shoving her away without
regard for her feelings. Lena nodded as a kind smile made its way to
her lips, looking at him, cold and volatile, from behind.

"...Bete Loga, make sure you come back. I'll be waiting for you."

And then she clung to his back, hugging him tightly.

Closing her eyes, she relished his warmth spreading across her
cheek—though he elbowed her, jabbing her with a vicious blow and
sending her flying with a squeal.

"Hey, that Amazon keeps yapping on about Aisha...Do you think
she's caught on to the shady stuff our familia's doing, Asfi?"

"It's not any worse than your big mouth, Lulune. Meaning it'll just
be an even bigger headache for me. Don't you worry..."

Hermes Familia's group watched Bete and Lena's boisterous back-and-forth from afar.

As the chienthrope girl tapped her shoulder, Asfi readjusted her glasses, attempting to hide the mounting fatigue around her eyes, blue hair billowing. The war tiger Falgar, the prum Merrill, and all the other members of their familia looked at her with gazes filled with pity.

"I know we formed an alliance and all, which means we don't have a choice but to join the first attack...That said, it's a real bummer. Disabling the traps is one thing, but telling us to map this stupidly huge dungeon, too? Like isn't this place crazy dangerous?" Lulune complained despondently.

"All we have to do is follow *Loki Familia* and *stealthily investigate* the paths they clear: nothing more, nothing less. It's a simple task. Relax. Your shoulders are tense," Asfi responded with a sigh as she adjusted her mind-set.

The right arm of Hermes understood the importance of this preliminary skirmish. So while she hid it behind the facade of the sage leader, she was also bracing herself.

"Besides...we've got powerful reinforcements."

Glancing aside, she spotted a masked adventurer wearing a deep hood behind her—a single elf who was standing there quietly.

"Lefiya!"

"Miss Filvis!" Lefiya called out toward Filvis, who was darting in her direction through the squad lining up in front of the southwest entrance. "You're in this squad, too?"

"Yes, since I'm Lord Dionysus's guard. It's wonderful that you ended up being here, too—"

Just as they were ready to bask in their good luck, someone else broke in, cutting off Filvis. "Lord Dionysus's guard, huh? Look at you, pretending to be his right-hand woman. All you did was gain his sympathy and monopolize his affection by playing the victim of the misfortune on the twenty-seventh floor."

"Aura..."

As with the two of them, it was another elf with venom practically dripping from every word. She had sweeping white locks that were tied up, the exact opposite of Filvis's black hair. Her eyes were a deep purple, and she might have been a year or two older than the pair.

Cloaking her body were her battle clothes, black and red, as she held a long staff that marked her as a magic user. It was an unconventional one, seemingly based on the flower known as the queen of the night. It was almost possible to see her fussy nature, a quality she shared with other elves. Put another way, she seemed to have a high-strung sort of hostility.

Aura Moriel. *Dionysus Familia*'s second-in-command. A Level 2. Alias: Krater. She had joined the familia at the same time as Filvis, and they should have been the two most senior members in their group. At least, that was what Lefiya remembered from when she'd looked up the members of *Dionysus Familia* back when their familias had first formed an alliance.

"I thought you were taking him away and moving around in secret. Come to find you've managed to get the whole familia wrapped up in it…Are you going to kill us this time, Banshee?"

"…!" Lefiya recoiled at the nickname.

This was referring to Filvis, because every party that she had joined ever since the Twenty-Seventh-Floor Nightmare had been entirely wiped out, leaving her as the sole survivor. Lefiya knew she was still despised internally as the elf who killed her party, despite being the leader of *Dionysus Familia*.

"…I'm sorry, Aura," Filvis responded under her critical gaze and offered nothing else.

On the day of the incident six years back, Aura had apparently been left off the party. Filvis must have felt obliged to her for slinking back to the familia, alive, after letting the then-leader and all the senior members perish. And Aura almost certainly did blame her—to the point that their differences couldn't be settled even six years later.

It was further complicated by the fact that Aura adored Dionysus just as much as Filvis loved him—Filvis, who had the seat next to

Dionysus under her control and who had been appointed the current leader of the familia. Aura couldn't even hide the contempt toward her in her voice.

It wasn't hard to imagine why Filvis distanced herself from the familia, given her feelings and everything else.

As Filvis looked down, Lefiya was starting to object.

"…But just this once, we'll set aside the pointless antagonism."

"What?"

Both Lefiya and Filvis were shocked. Despite her obvious reluctance, Aura was clear in her declaration.

"I understand the situation. And Lord Dionysus even said it himself. This is for the sake of our comrades who were killed…There is no reason to slight fellow familia members on pointless pretexts."

"Aura…"

"Let's try our best to not get in *Loki Familia*'s way. And you: Make sure you perform your duty—and not just cling to your kin."

On that snide note, Aura spun on her heel and made it clear that they would provide their support. Lefiya was thrilled for Filvis—that she'd been acknowledged by her own familia for all that she'd accomplished.

"I'm happy for you, Miss Filvis." Lefiya smiled.

"…Yes." Filvis grinned back—a mix of gratitude to her fellow elf who had approached her after those long years and sadness at making Aura forgive her.

"Are they gonna be okay? Your kids?"

"Filvis has a wall up between her and the rest of the members. But it looks like, at least this once, they've settled their differences. Aura is a wise girl. She won't bring her personal feelings to an operation that bears the fate of the city."

Watching their exchange from afar, Loki expressed some doubt, but Dionysus just brushed back his hair with flair. His words had the faint ring of a god bragging about his precious followers. Loki stuck out her tongue at his pretentious air.

"If ye ask me, I'd be more inclined to wonder if having you two along will really be okay…"

"Sorry, Gareth! But there'll definitely be a point where we're gonna have to be here! Guaranteed!…Probably! Make sure you do a good job protectin' us!"

Gareth had butted into their conversation. The dwarf had been given command of the southwestern squad, fully equipped with a helmet and heavy armor, narrowing his eyes as he peeled the annoyingly warm arms of his patron goddess off his shoulders.

Both Loki and Dionysus were joining the fray for this first strike. They had judged that a god's power would be necessary in order to corner Thanatos, who was leading the Evils' Remnants, and Enyo, who was suspected of being the mastermind behind it all.

"My apologies, Elgarm. Feel free to use my familia members to your heart's content. Of course, the same goes for me. As I said, my familia is united again, just this once." Dionysus's eyes sharpened. "In order to avenge my followers."

His eyes normally never showed any emotions, but they revealed his divine will, clear and intense. As Gareth responded with silence, Loki stood next to him and looked into the god's eyes. She fished something out of her pocket and tossed it to him.

"Just in case…take that."

She'd thrown a single crystal to Dionysus. Unlike a natural one, this one had a mysterious light shimmering inside it. Loki was holding another one in her own hand.

"…Thank you, Loki."

After his eyes widened in realization, he grinned at the goddess who was looking at him with a surly look on her face.

"—Everyone, stand to."

Finn kept it short as he announced the start of the operation.

Before Knossos's northeast entrance, the familia members standing around the prum holding his long spear adopted tense looks and fighting spirits. Finn did not give a speech to raise morale as he had before the expedition. It was unnecessary. His sharp gaze was all it took. He looked down at his hand. It held a small crystal, just like the ones in Loki's and Dionysus's palms.

Upon checking that the magic item was giving off a light, he raised his head to face the tightly shut orichalcum gate and roared: "Commence the operation!"

The familia member at the head of the group raised the key, opening the gate.

With a battle cry, the adventurers charged into Knossos.

"It's time."

As the adventurers' shouts resounded from the magic item—the oculus—and thundering footsteps rang out, Fels looked up.

The Dungeon's eighteenth floor. "Night" had fallen in the Under Resort.

The crystals clinging to the ceiling like chrysanthemums were silent. Unlike during the day, the entire floor was totally shrouded in darkness, where the shadows of monsters writhed around.

The armed Xenos had gathered at the floor's eastern edge in front of the entrance to Knossos. They were receiving information from Fels's oculus. Gareth and the leaders of the other squads had them, too, to collectively respond when the signal began. Closing the gap between the Dungeon and the surface, the allied forces of humans and monsters began their assault from all directions.

The armored lizardman's claws ripped into the ground; the gargoyle spread his stony wings; the siren mirrored his movements.

Fels gave the command.

"Let's put an end to this chain of battles—*Go!*"

The monsters howled as they loped into the demons' lair.

"Garuaaaaaaaaaaaaaaaaaaaaaagh!" belted the wild werewolf, exterminating anything blocking his path.

A swarm of vargs, vividly colored monsters in the shape of water spiders, literally exploded from the impact of his fierce kicks.

"Don't get shaken off by Bete! Push forward!"

Led by Anakity, *Loki Familia* hurried down the path while Bete scattered the wall of monsters with the strength of his charge. Letting Bete be the wedge that forced open the way through the large passage, the lovely catgirl cut down the monsters flowing out of the side paths as she sprinted past them. And if any happened to get past the two of them, there was a stream of Level-3 adventurers behind them ready to slaughter any survivors. The relentless *thud* of combat boots continued, leaving corpses of monsters that were nothing more than sacks of blood, vibrant magic stones beyond count, and swirling dunes of ash in their wake.

Knossos's first floor. The southeast.

The instant the door opened, the squad storming the labyrinth charged in at full speed, loosing the opening shot of the battle. They swept away the remnants of the Evils who were lying in wait, breaking through in one fell swoop—as if their pent-up hatred and rage exploded out as they rushed into Knossos.

The familia members had been told the details of the operation by Finn: an assault but, more importantly, a reconnaissance in force. Even if the second attack would be the real deal, once they set foot in the enemy base, there was no reason for them not to run wild. In addition to mapping as much of the vast dungeon as possible, they were striking at major facilities of their enemies.

There were two priorities that overrode everything else: The first was discovering the demi-spirit. And the second was securing the enemy's ringleaders. In this case, that meant Barca, who they expected to have inherited the blueprints to Knossos, and Thanatos, the patron god of the remnants of the Evils.

If they succeeded in capturing them, they would get a much better layout of the labyrinth and contribute significantly to neutralizing the Evils. As with all bodies—living beings or organizations—once the head was bashed in, the rest would cease to be a threat.

Finn had said that speed would be of the utmost importance on this first strike. They would not give the enemy any time to reorganize, let alone to counterattack. This attack would effectively put the last nail in the coffin—crushing the strength of the Evils' side.

Following their captain's order—and, more importantly, to get revenge for their fallen friends—*Loki Familia* surged forward.

"There's a door straight ahead in the back and another to the right!"

"Open the one to the right first!"

"It reeks of people here! Don't get yourself killed from a trap!" Bete yelled as he dismantled a monster with the Dual Roland blades he was wielding in either hand.

"Same to you. Match my timing!" Anakity fired back immediately.

The Daedalus Orb that she held unlocked the door, and as Bete warned, the Evils' Remnants on the other side fired at once. Anticipating this attack, Bete absorbed the magic with his Frosvirt boots while Anakity and the others took advantage of the small opening to slip through and slice into the enemy squad.

"Wha—?!"

In the blink of an eye, the Remnants fell into chaos. From the first-tier adventurer with his preeminent battle strength down, *Loki Familia* proceeded to incapacitate the enemy forces. Using magic and magical blades to deal with those who tried to use explosive devices to take them out in a suicide charge, they mercilessly let their fanatical enemies blow themselves up before they could get close enough to do any damage.

The squad in the southeast, which was centered around Bete, was composed mostly of animal people. They could make good use of their enhanced senses to perceive traps and detect the layout of the labyrinth. They were the main mapping squad. The hume bunny Rakuta, who had joined the Fairy Force last time, was in that group, making full use of her skills. During the past operation, she had trailblazed this southeastern part of Knossos with Riveria, so she was navigating for the group as they rushed forward.

"Hurry up with that pillar! Don't lose sight of Aki and Bete's team!"

The follow-up group led by Raul immediately reinforced the door that Bete had opened, erecting three metal pillars in between the doors that opened vertically to act as braces to prop them open. This way, they guaranteed that the doors could not be closed remotely, ensuring the squad would not get separated. Even if the orichalcum doors were indestructible, that meant nothing if they could not be closed, and their weight was not enough to break pillars made from high-grade metal.

Those pillars were one of the items that Finn and the others had gathered during the intervening ten days, a crucial tool for taking on Knossos.

—Meanwhile, in the southwest.

"Set up a base! Mappers, spread out from there as you work!"

The squad led by Gareth was setting up pillars, too.

Given that the gates were constructed from the extremely rare material orichalcum, there was a very low probability that there would be a bunch of them. Any reasonable person would put doors at the important points on a route.

Once they could ensure the safety of the surroundings, they used the pillars as a base and unleashed the mappers.

"Make sure you stay with an escort! Don't make the people from *Dionysus Familia* do it themselves! Cruz and Narfi, I'm sure the enemy will start pressuring our lines of retreat! I'm leaving the rear to you!"

""Yes, sir!""

Aura and the other members of *Dionysus Familia* thoroughly investigated the labyrinth, accompanied by Level-3 or higher members of *Loki Familia*. The secondary force members, Narfi and Cruz, responded to Gareth's instructions, while he watched out for enemy ambushes.

They continued to open new ground, stopping when they encountered a door or dead end, while Gareth and the others were in the process of holding off and then routing the big wave of enemies pressing from the front.

"Mr. Gareth! The group that went right at the last crossroad found a stairway that goes down!"

"Well done! We're heading there!"

His voice boomed out at the report as he wheeled the squad around. The southwest squad quickly moved to the next floor as they continued to map.

"Aaaaaaaah?!" shrieked someone from the northeast squad.

"Olba?!"

Knocking down enemies left and right at the head of the group, Tiona suddenly swung around in shock. The enemy's ambush had hit their lines right from the side, and more and more people were starting to shrink back as those who were cut were unable to stem the flow of blood.

"E-enemies! And they all have cursed weapons!" reported a girl in a shrill voice, causing worry to ripple through the squad.

The combat strength of the lower-tier forces of the Evils was low. At most, they were Level 2. As long as they were careful of the violas, even *Dionysus Familia* members could handle them. The only problem was that they were wielding cursed weapons. They had to draw blood only once.

Cursed weapons. The unhealable damnation that had stolen some lives from *Loki Familia*. A single scratch from one of those ominous pitch-black blades would be deadly, an unavoidable depletion of *Loki Familia*'s fighting strength.

The remnants of the Evils shouted. With bloodshot eyes, they looked as if they were possessed by death itself. Facing the adventurers who tried to protect those who had been wounded, they devoted themselves to landing a single swing with the curse, even if they were forced to trade blows.

"Healing droplets, tears of light, eternal sanctuary—"

But even that accursed suicide rush was thwarted by her holy hymn.

"Five-meter perimeter. All casualties are inside the area of effect. Activating."

There was a single healer at the back of the squad, protecting the adventurers as she chanted.

With her platinum hair fluttering in the light of the magic power that she generated, Amid unleashed her magic. *"Dia Frater!"*

A magic circle in the shape of a diamond appeared on the stone floor. It was as if a pure white splendor had sprung to life, healing all the wounds of *Loki Familia*'s members—even the cursed wounds that should have been unhealable. The Evils were aghast at the sight as the adventurers cheered in wonder.

Her magic healed *everything*. It literally healed all wounds, restored stamina, and managed to boost all Status conditions. Curses were no exception. Essentially, it was a means of complete recovery. If she poured enough power into it, her magic was influenced by her Enigma ability and could even heal faster than an elixir, the ultimate healing item. Even Riveria, who was hailed as the city's greatest mage, could not begin to match Amid when it came to healing capabilities.

"I will heal everything. And I shall destroy all traces of the curse. Please fight to your hearts' content."

Amid Teasanare. Dea Saint. The city's greatest healer, who was capable of outlasting even a being of immeasurable power, including a Monster Rex.

"Amid, you're awesome!"

"Since you put it so nicely, I'll take you up on that...! Let's gooooooooo!"

Under all normal circumstances, a healer should hang around in the back of the group. Thanks to the efforts of that lone healer, the adventurers' morale catapulted. As Tiona shouted, Tione licked her lips and leaped out with her, slashing into the enemy forces with her Kukri knives. The Evils could do nothing more than despair as the sisters overran them.

One of the supplies that Finn and the others had pushed hardest to get was the anti-curse medicine. With the enemy capable of spreading an unhealable affliction, it became critical that all the squads have a supply of anti-curse medicine. It was logical to prepare a lot of it in case of unforeseen situations. In the limited time frame that they had to prepare, they neglected to acquire the amount of

© Kiyotaka Haimura

preplanned medicine for even one squad, though the shortened timeline wasn't the only reason.

That was why Amid had come. She was the one woman in all of Orario who could lift the curse using magic.

"Dea Saint…! Was she always this absurd of a healer?!"

"Even though she's not a mage, there's a magic circle…No friggin' way."

From her position at the center of the group, Alicia groaned involuntarily as Elfie, who had never seen Amid get serious before, forgot where she was for a moment. Even as a veteran, Alicia had never seen a healer functioning as an offensive force and not just a support one.

But Amid's confounding abilities didn't stop there. With a single spell, the shining magic circle morphed into a barrier of light, maintaining a zone where all her allies would continue to be healed. It completely outweighed the damage caused by the Evils desperately trying to fight back. To the Evils, the scene of their enemies' wounds healing in the blink of an eye must have been nothing short of a nightmare.

But if the Evils were bringing an uncurable malady to the table, they would bring immortality.

The vanguard was freed from the cumbersome task of dealing with items on an individual level. Attack and advance. That was all they needed to do now.

Though she never worked toward gaining the ability of a mage, there was a magic circle at Amid's feet, raising the power of her spell. With her robes billowing as she released rays of holy light, she was the embodiment of the Enigma ability. If someone said that she was a goddess reborn, everyone would have believed it.

"'If I'm there, you need not worry about burning through items,' huh? If anyone else was making that claim, I'd brush them off as reckless, but…you're quite the healer," commented Finn, repeating her assurance as he spectated the raging battle, tapping the shaft of his spear against his shoulder with a smile.

It was unbelievable to think that in the northeast squad, exposed to the most intense counterattack of all the parties that invaded Knossos, all the healing was being handled by Amid alone. The two other girls from *Dian Cecht Familia* were waiting at her side as if they were holy woman's attendants, eyes closed as they preserved their Mind.

Amid was handling the entire party. She had received the title of Dea Saint from the gods because she could maintain the battle lines against a floor boss *by herself.* That meant she was more than able to keep up with the needs of a large party alone.

"As the person commanding the squad, this is a convenient arrangement for me, but is your Mind going to be okay, Amid?"

"I will be fine. I have enough potions. Even without a resupply, I can assure that it would be sufficient to continue at this rate for a distance equivalent to going down to around the twentieth floor of the Dungeon."

Standing next to Amid in the shining white magic circle, Finn smiled wryly at her response. He was seriously considering asking Dian Cecht to borrow her for the next expedition, but he switched gears and started giving out orders.

"The attacks from the enemy are weakening. We're going to switch from our defensive positions to advancing. Please get ready."

"Understood."

Gazing out over the battlefield with a penetrating gaze, the healer bowed piously, as if she had reached the same conclusion as Finn.

Right as Finn was about to move ahead, she called to him. "Captain Finn. I can maintain the battle line, but I cannot foresee how the battle will progress. Do you believe the operation is progressing smoothly?"

Amid had sworn to prevent any victims from sacrificing their lives in this operation.

Finn glanced back. "If I said that we will totally overwhelm them at this rate...well, that would be wishful thinking. There's no way that Knossos would fall from this much. They still have the creatures," he responded with his unvarnished opinion.

Looking away from Amid as she listened in silence, Finn stabbed his spear into the devil sculpture built into the labyrinth wall—piercing it right in its eye.

"But we can't afford to lose. This time, we'll win."

The visual information from the eye's range of sight cut out. Thanatos smiled at the prum's blue eyes staring at them through the eye, but then it ceased to function.

"They've broken in from the northeast, southeast, and southwest doors on the first floor!"

"They're advancing too fast! They annihilated all the monsters and our dispatched soldiers…!"

"H-have they already advanced to the second floor?! What the hell is going on?!"

A tumult unlike any other roiled all around him.

The labyrinth master's room in the depths of Knossos.

The space could be called the Evils' base. It was filled with the incessant shrieks of Thanatos's followers, pessimistic and badly shaken. Not unreasonably. They were currently being invaded. They were facing *Loki Familia*'s attack—what seemed like an all-out assault from an alliance of familias. The fate of their dearest wishes would be impacted by the results of this fight. In other words, it would determine the victors and the vanquished.

"They prepared for this, huh…I guess we earned ourselves a disadvantage by letting them escape Knossos once," Thanatos muttered to himself as he looked down at the watery screen spread across the central pedestal, at the transmitted information from the eyes placed all around the labyrinth.

Obviously, their enemies were able to control the doors using the keys they had found, but they had even prepared a response to the cursed weapons and all the various traps. They had Barca, the descendant of Daedalus, to control the doors and activate traps from a distance, but *Loki Familia* was searching out and destroying their eyes—the observation mechanisms embedded in the sculptures' eyes and wall reliefs—whenever they found them. Without the ability to track the enemy's movements, they could not effectively activate the traps from afar.

Loki Familia's ignominious defeat in the first attack and the Fairy Force's surprise attack were the cornerstones for this assault. They had examined all the information gathered from those operations and applied them to their current strategy.

Scrutinizing the profile of the prum hero through the screen, Thanatos could not help but be filled with wonder and admiration, even though he was the enemy.

"L-Lord Thanatos?! We can't stop their advance…! It's not just the monsters! We're losing our comrades, too! At this rate…!"

"We gathered the keys from all the children who went out on the front lines, right? As long as the enemy does not steal any more of them, everything will be fine. As long as there are orichalcum doors blocking the way, the enemy can only split up so much."

They had retrieved the keys from the soldiers deployed all around the maze and gathered them in the labyrinth master's room. With their stronghold invaded, they desperately needed to avoid the enemy stealing any more keys, just like the Fairy Force had done. The more keys the enemy had, the more they would be able to do as they pleased in Knossos. That was why the Evils had taken that precaution. It had been a last resort because it prevented the free movement of their own forces, even if Barca could control the doors from his spot.

Currently, the only people allowed to carry a key were Thanatos and Levis. With the possibility of running into Loki Familia and being defeated in an instant hanging over their heads, not even the commanders were excepted from that rule.

Planting both hands on his pedestal, Thanatos swayed his crossed legs back and forth. The commander who had come to report to him looked shocked as the god maintained his usual composure despite the gravity of the situation.

"More than that, I'm curious about their speed—it's like they have a one-track mind."

Thanatos glanced again at the adventurer displayed on the

pedestal. At that rate of advance, they had to be scheming to pressure the head of the organization. More than that, Braver must have had an estimate on the location of the demi-spirit.

Thanatos's eyes suddenly narrowed. "Do we know how many routes the enemy came in from and where?"

"Y-yes, sir. Three parties from the first floor, every entrance save the northwest. And the monsters are attacking from the eighteenth floor onward."

"Ikelos's toys, huh…? Braver joining hands with those monsters. That was totally outside my expectations…If there are advances from the lowest and highest floors…I wonder if he's planning a pincer."

Covering his androgynous face with his long fingers, Thanatos descended into deep thought. *There are currently four enemy units… They stole two keys from us during the last fight, plus the two from those heretical monsters with the vouivre…It adds up, but…*

From the battle before in Daedalus Street, he'd anticipated this amount of fighters, based on what he knew about *Loki Familia* and the Xenos. But Thanatos was concerned.

There was a lost key they had not been able to track down—

"Lord Thanatos?! A new enemy party has appeared on the twelfth floor!"

"—As I feared." Ignoring the shouts of his subordinates, the god allowed a nihilistic smile to appear on his face as he turned around. "Who's in the group?"

As Thanatos gazed at the scene displayed on the pedestal, the messenger paled as he shouted in reply.

"It's Nine Hell! And the Sword Princess!"

"Tempest!" Aiz fully unleashed her Airiel as she stepped into the labyrinth.

"Keep up with Aiz as if your life depended on it!"

""Yes, ma'am!"" shouted the familia members in unison behind Riveria.

As if being propelled by their voices, Aiz rushed through the stone-paved passage. She held out the key gripped in her right hand and opened the giant door blocking her path. It was the one that Cruz had received in the bargain with Hermes, the Daedalus Orb that Freya had secretly taken when Ishtar was sent back to the heavens. The final key that the Evils, including their late leader, Valletta Grede, had failed to track down.

The appearance of a fifth party was an unexpected blow to the Evils, who had thought that there were only four squads taking part in the assault.

"Aiz, don't worry if we start to get separated! Just run wild!"

"Okay!"

This force was made up of only members of *Loki Familia*—consisting of elves, including Riveria, all Level 3 or higher and nimble on their feet. Aiz pushed ahead by herself in front of that party, which had been formed for its dexterity, opening the doors she came across and slicing deeper into the labyrinth with unbelievable speed.

"Don't overlook even the slightest abnormalities! If something reacts to Aiz's wind—that's our number one priority!"

Aiz's role in this operation was to act as a radar. The one who inherited the blood of spirits was unleashing her magic over a wide range, running around through the labyrinth in order to catch any reaction by the corrupted spirit.

Finn predicted the demi-spirit would be somewhere on the eighth, ninth, or tenth floor…! In Knossos's middle levels!

Finn had calculated that it was likely that the demi-spirit was tucked away somewhere on Knossos's middle-level floors, based on the reports from Riveria's Fairy Force. When she had broken through all the way to the twelfth floor, she had noticed that the enemy soldiers and monsters were deployed with the greatest density on the eighth through tenth floors.

Along with Finn, the rest of the fighters and the Xenos were the units charged with clearing the labyrinth and chasing the ringleaders, while Aiz and the others were the secret squad searching for wherever the ticking time bomb of a demi-spirit was hiding.

They let some time pass after Finn invaded before launching their surprise attack from the entrance on the Dungeon's twelfth floor that they had already found.

—*Listen up, Aiz.*

—*It's imperative to find the demi-spirit, but in the worst case,* it's fine *even if you don't find it.*

—*All you need to do is…*

Aiz remembered the orders Finn had given her before the operation. In addition to acting as a radar, she had another crucial role.

"I will…lure her out!"

"Aria?" Levis furrowed her brow. She was getting ready to go out and annihilate the invaders when she received this report.

"Y-yes! The Sword Princess and Nine Hell's party has come in from the twelfth floor!" The soldier sent by the Evils prattled on in a mix of fear and impatience. "Lord Thanatos has declared th-that they should be prioritized…!"

"…Oh, that's what he's after," she spat back in annoyance.

She understood what the soldier was saying before he could even finish. She correctly realized that Aiz was trying to uncover where the spirits were located. Levis knew that Aiz's wind at full power could act as a radar. Once, during the last time she was in Knossos, Aiz had done the drastic move of summoning an unbelievably strong wind to let her scattered comrades know where she was. The spirits would react to Aiz's wind, even from all the way across the floor. And once they started bawling, they were not easily calmed, giving the enemy a critical hint as to where they were located.

From Knossos's perspective, letting Aiz's squad move as they pleased was not an option. And no one other than Levis would be capable of dealing with her.

"Is drawing my attention to Aria part of their plan…?"

Levis, who had been heading toward the adventurers running wild on the upper floors, changed course.

This is definitely one of that prum's schemes.

Picturing the face of the man who had stood against her several times, Levis scoffed and darted to the twelfth floor toward Aiz's squad.

"The Evils and the creature will be forced to respond to Aiz," Finn explained as his group rushed along. "In fact, *that was precisely why* I had Riveria take command of that team. Both as someone who has rampaged in this labyrinth before and as someone capable of taking the reins and guiding Aiz, she was the only one who could lead them."

"That means Aiz and the others are…"

"They will effectively be bait. If the creature heads out to counter them, the risk of the other squads getting defeated decreases considerably."

Finn revealed his plan to Amid, who was dashing next to him. With Tione taking the lead of the vanguards and Tiona and the others promptly mowing down the monsters coming out of the countless crossroads, his brain kept spinning in thought.

"If the creature comes to us, then we'll retreat at full speed. If we can stall for time, Aiz's wind will be able to find the location of the demi-spirit."

Finn had left Thanatos and Levis with one of two choices. It was up to them to decide. Finn judged that they would choose the former and counter Aiz, but in the event they *lost their cool*, he could not be sure what they would do. That was why he had prepared the parties for suitable responses. The initial preparations were to avoid getting wiped out even if they were routed.

He wasn't pursuing a result with minimized losses: He was aiming for one with no losses at all. He was not planning to abandon anyone. He could not say whether that change was growth or regression. But the precipitous tightrope of chasing ideals was far more difficult, stressful, and meaningful than the easy route of assuming they would sustain casualties from the start.

In the event that he failed, no losses would turn into minimal losses. And if he succeeded, he would achieve his ideal. That was why Braver chose the harder route. After everything that had happened, that was how Finn was thinking now.

If Loki were there, she would surely have said that it was a definite growth on Finn's part.

"Either way, it's going to be a race against time."

The man-made labyrinth, Knossos, stretched all the way down halfway through the Dungeon's middle levels. Faced with that enormous amount of ground to cover, Finn had not chosen a drawn-out battle or a war of attrition—he had chosen a short, decisive battle.

"Run! Advance! As far and as fast as you can! This will chip away at the enemy's life span!"

""Sir!!""

Finn shouted encouragement to the whole group while keeping the healers in reserve, ready to spring into action.

"I found an entrance to the Dungeon!"

"Keep pushing! Calculate where we are, you useless rabbit!"

"Y-yes, sir!"

A single blow crumbled the rock face, opening a stone path to the real Dungeon. Bete howled at the adventurers who had reached the open gate first while Rakuta scrambled to open a map of the Dungeon. Based on the characteristic terrain, she narrowed it down, announcing, "We're on the Dungeon's third floor, the northeast section!"

Knossos's third floor. The animal-people squad, which was centered on Bete, had rushed down the floors at a wild pace, making it "outside." It wasn't a path leading to a lower level or the location of the spirits but passages connecting to the Dungeon that would be helpful when it was time to withdraw. Bete was making sure to increase their options.

They'd connected to a part of the Dungeon that was a simple light-blue labyrinth. Considering where they were on the Knossos side, it was almost certainly the third floor.

The small room that the passage opened into just happened to have some lower-class adventurers hunting monsters at the edge of the floor. Everyone was dumbstruck seeing *Loki Familia* appear from the broken wall and stood there slack-jawed, paralyzed, including the goblins they were hunting. As the Level-1 party crumbled into confusion, the Level-6 werewolf roared, "This ain't a damn show! Scram!" sending them scurrying from the room screaming "W-we're sorrrrrrrrry?!" They were shoulder to shoulder with the monsters as they ran.

"I'm going ahead! You take care of this shit! If you're useless and can't catch up, you'll get left behind!" barked the werewolf.

"Geez, I got it! Morel! Head aboveground from here and contact the *Ganesha* and *Hermes Familia* reserves! Prepare to run a supply line through this area!"

"Understood!"

Bete's instructions hurled abuse at her, causing the catgirl to snap back at him.

While Bete stayed at the leading edge of the squad, wielding his savage breakthrough ability, the second-in-command and effective leader, Anakity, fired off orders in his stead. While setting up pillars so that the gate could not be lowered, she sent a Level-2 member of *Loki Familia*'s reserves to deliver the message. Not watching as Morel disappeared into the Dungeon, she chased after Bete, who had already started pushing forward along a different route.

"—Please accept this offering! Lord Thanatooooos!"

Meanwhile, in the trailing group behind Bete's advance.

Before Raul could direct his team, one of the God of Death's followers set off a chain of suicide bombs.

"Urgh…?!"

"Gaaaaaaah…?!"

Because they had thoroughly prepared for suicide bombings beforehand, there was no direct damage. However, after the explosion died down, the smell of burned flesh wafting up, the scattered limbs and the horrific corpses left behind caused some of the younger girls in the familia to hunch over and start vomiting. The same was true for some of the members of *Dionysus Familia* who had joined them as mappers.

"Gah...Don't throw up! Stand! If we slow down, that will affect Bete and his squad! Don't look away! Fight!" bellowed Raul, in charge of this group, as he clenched his fists, struggling to find the words to say.

Yanking the arm of a familia member on all fours on the floor, he forced the squad to keep moving. He was desperate to accomplish his assigned task, even as he fought the nausea choking him at the back of his own throat.

This is different from a battle in the normal Dungeon or a fight between familias...! This is the real Evils! The enemy who clashed against the captain and the others! The battlefield where so many...so many of the people in the familia before us perished!

When he had first joined the familia, the rookie Raul had not been sent out to fight during the most heated period of the clashes with the Evils. By the time Raul and Anakity had started being part of the fighting forces, it was the end stages of the Dark Ages, after the alliance of familias had been formed under the Guild's jurisdiction.

Raul had never known such an inhuman battlefield. Lives were mercilessly cast aside. Rendering the enemy powerless without killing them was an impossibility. The battlefield did not tolerate hypocrites.

He rushed through the charred passage.

It was almost like an actual war where trench warfare, sieges, suppression, and everything else was abound. They would be forced to pay the price in order to bring down the enemy's base. The work of men was all around them, even though it should have had nothing to do with adventurers whose job was to scour the Dungeon.

"Set up the pillars! Monsters are coming from the path to the right! Walls assemble! Stall for time! Ines and the other mages, start casting! Watch out for the violas!"

Despite all that, Raul put his all into maintaining control of the situation. He knew that if he was shaken, the party would lose steam. He trusted that his desperate voice would be a source of courage for the other familia members.

In truth, Raul's quavering orders and his face, which was as pale as anyone else's, could not even remotely be mistaken for those of a charismatic commander, but—they gritted their teeth.

If even Raul can still be in high spirits, then so can I. That thought pushed the young familia members to roughly wipe the vomit from their mouths, raising their spirits and bringing them to start moving again.

It gives me courage, too…! Seeing the captain's back when he leads everyone!

Raul tried to embody the small back that was always in front of him with his own, raging as he cut down the enemy's resisting forces.

"Shield me, cleansing chalice—Dio Grail!"

A shield of white light cut off a violent explosion closing in.

"Filvis, speed up your casts! What if Lord Dionysus got injured?!"

"I'm doing it as fast as I can! Why don't you try counterattacking some while mapping, Aura?!"

"S-stop it, you two! Don't fight each other—fight them, please!"

As *Dionysus Familia*'s leader and second-in-command argued, Lefiya shouted back with a hint of grumbling in her voice as she fired off a blast. They were on the third floor of Knossos on the front line, where the number of Evils members and monsters was gradually increasing, and the counterattack was getting more intense.

"Raaaaaaaaaaah!"

Leaving aside the elves who were on edge from the increased resistance they were encountering, the stout dwarf Gareth pushed forward.

Faced with *Loki Familia*'s strongest wrecking ball charging at them with two great shields at the ready, other than catching the tiniest fear of death, Thanatos's followers did not hesitate to set off a chain of explosions.

"*Tch*, I really hate this kind of fight…but at least it's easier to keep moving when they're quick to give up on an actual battle."

Not shaken in the least as he withstood the explosion blasting against his shield, Gareth was furious at the enemy force for not even trying to face them. But from another perspective, if the enemy blew themselves up, they were as good as abandoning the battle.

The force of the explosions was menacing, but those same ones caused a battle line to crumble that otherwise would have been able to hold out longer. Their advance was still moving smoothly, albeit in proportion to the damage that their squad was taking from the enemies.

"…They're reeeeally consistent about blowing themselves up. As soon as we get a certain distance away, it's an insta-boom."

"Yes. They must fear us capturing them. It might be to prevent us from learning the key points in Knossos…"

Loki and Dionysus stood in the rear guard, behind stout soldiers. Their gods' eyes saw through what the Evils were trying to accomplish. When aiming to get a grasp of all the enemy's infrastructure, the simplest method was to get it from interrogating captives. It didn't matter if the enemy was tight-lipped; there would be someone who would break if they were willing to use whatever methods were necessary.

Thanatos was removing that possibility at the root by using suicide bombs as an attack and means of silencing them. It was a desperate measure to prevent more information from getting out, but it was also causing real damage to his forces. It was a tactic that could be used only by the God of Death, who had promised his followers a future beyond their demise.

"Finn said that speed was going to be crucial, but…we're taking casualties just pushing forward. We might run out of ways to recover at this rate. Guess we won't be able to make our way across that tightrope." Loki licked her lips as she slightly opened her crimson eyes.

"But the same goes for them, too."

"—Aaaaaaaaaaaaaaaaaaah!"
"Gah?!"

The vargs flinched at the thunderous sound wave. The lizardman with a sword in either hand mercilessly cut into the vividly colored monsters that continued gushing out, as if trying to stop their charge or at least slow their advance.

"There, next!"

"Advance! Advance!"

"Aaaaaaaaaaah!"

The group of armed Xenos was fighting, unleashing an unending stream of shouts mixed with human words. Wielding a strength that could easily slaughter the vargs and violas, they were undoubtedly a menacing enemy to the forces defending Knossos. They were just a single party, but they were advancing even faster than *Loki Familia*.

"Rei, which path?!"

"Right at the next crossroad! That leads to a new room!"

The monsters' senses surpassed the average adventurer's, but the main reason they had an acute awareness of their surroundings was thanks to the echolocation that the siren Rei was using. With the ability to create high-frequency sound waves, her inhuman technique let her understand the complicated construction of the labyrinth. She led the band of Xenos farther and farther, unstopped by doors and never caught by the roaming swarms of enemies. Conveying what she said, the lizardman Lido at the front of the group had his comrades swing around.

"—! Lido, a plant!"

"Great! Let's crush it!"

A grotesque organ in the shape of an upside-down funnel was enshrined in the middle of the large room. Composed of a green meat, the plant had crystals that resembled the ones on vargs scattered through it. The inner part in the center was giving off a flickering light with the appearance of a living organism's beating heart, like a crushed pomegranate or an egg.

There was a green carpet unfurled across the floor, and several vargs were born from the sticky ooze seeping from the egg in the center. The gargoyle's voice and the lizardman's order overlapped as the red-cap goblin, harpy, troll, and all the monsters proceeded to overrun the room.

But it didn't matter how many vividly colored monsters it could produce—the plant did not have any real means of defending itself, broken beyond repair in the blink of an eye.

"That's the fourth one! There'll be no end to it at this rate…!"

The Xenos burned with rage. Their grudge against the brutal hunters of *Ikelos Familia*—who had captured their brethren and were the root of all that evil—was in some ways even greater than the adventurers' own. That was the cause of their billowing force, which surpassed even *Loki Familia*'s.

Because *Loki Familia*'s attack was splitting up the Evils' human forces, it was mostly just monsters positioned in the lower levels of Knossos. Put another way, because the Xenos were taking on all the monsters themselves and cutting off the supply lines from the lower levels' side, the burden on the adventurers rampaging through the middle levels and higher was significantly lessened. The unstoppable wave of the invasion teams composed of adventurers was an effect of the Xenos taking part in the fight.

The result of the incompatible monsters and humans fighting on different battlefields was greater than the sum of its parts, giving a glimpse of the tactical planning prowess of Finn, who had orchestrated all of it. With Finn and Fels working together, their prepared pincer attack was incredibly damaging to Knossos.

"Don't let your guard down, Lido."

"Yeah, I know! That reminds me. What happened to Fels? It's been a while…"

The golden-feathered siren fluttered down beside the excited lizardman. They were among the strongest of the Xenos and, together with the gargoyle Gros, the oldest group. Their relationship was similar to the one among Finn, Riveria, and Gareth in *Loki Familia*.

"Moving alone. Fels mentioned discovering some kind of monster storage vault, but…" Rei continued in a lowered voice. "Fels said it would not be long and to search for a path up to the next floor in this area in the meantime."

"Off planning some trick alone again, huh?! Can't be helped, I guess!"

"Also, we're allowed to go up to the *thirteenth floor*."

They were currently on Knossos's sixteenth floor, given permission to advance until right before the twelfth floor, where Aiz's group had burst in. The lizardman warrior bared his fangs. It was a ferocious smile, though only a certain boy among the humans could recognize it as one.

"Lido…are you going ahead?"

"Wiene…"

A dragon girl had overheard their conversation, approaching them—the vouivre who Bell had protected to the end and who Aiz had let go.

"I want to go, too. To the place where the goddess and Bell and the others live…I want to protect it, too!"

The dragon girl thought of a certain childish goddess and her followers as her beautiful amber eyes overflowed with resolve. She was humanoid, but beneath her black robe was the body of a full-fledged dragon. The girl had particularly enhanced senses, even relative to monsters—second only to Rei's echolocation when it came to sensing when something was off.

Wiene had volunteered for this dangerous mission herself. The girl who could do nothing as Bell protected her was nowhere to be seen. These monsters were just like people. They would fight for the sake of their bonds, for the things that were precious to them. Oddly, her figure was like a mirror image of Aiz once she hardened her resolve to battle.

"Wiene…All right, come! Together with the adventurers, we will protect Lady Hestia, too!"

"Yes!"

"Gros, we'll leave this to you! We are going to search a wider area!"

Leaving the cleanup of the remaining vividly colored monsters to the gargoyle's group, Lido, Wiene, and Rei moved out. The crimson stone in the vouivre's forehead flashed as she put all her effort into returning the favor she owed to the people aboveground.

"—! *She's coming!*" Riveria bellowed.

Riveria had a magic circle extended on standby as she followed behind Aiz, who was racing around. She had been maintaining the large-scale extermination spell—*Rea Laevateinn*—making sure it was ready to go at any moment. The jade magic circle reaching out from her feet could identify all obstructions, including distinguishing between enemies and allies.

The strong reaction that touched the outer edge of the circle, approaching at extreme speed, was without a doubt that of the creature. As soon as Riveria unleashed her warning, the squads were visibly on edge. Aiz was running at full speed at the head of the group, opening her eyes wide, and all of a sudden, she slammed the brakes hard enough to skid against the stone flooring.

"Pull back! All the way to the room where Arcus and the others are waiting! Hurry!"

They had continued advancing all the way until then, but at Riveria's order, they quickly started racing in the other direction. It was a complete retreat, like a wave pulling back into the sea. If Aiz was the radar to search out the location of the spirits and the lure to draw out Levis, then Riveria was the warning siren.

Though it gradually wore away at her Mind, she had kept the magic circle across an extraordinary range from the moment they entered Knossos. It was a measure taken to sense as soon as possible when their incomprehensibly powerful enemy was approaching, so as to quickly withdraw. That was why Riveria had been given command of that party—and why the city's strongest mage had been sent along with Aiz.

"Aiz, don't get ahead of yourself!"

"...I know!"

Having drawn out the creature, if Aiz tried to take her on one-on-one now, that would have been the worst possible strategy. At the very least, Finn would never allow it. Riveria ordered her to face Levis in the room where they had already positioned a fully armed and equipped squad.

Just this once, Aiz sealed off her fighting spirit, the strength she had gained while fighting the Warlord. Responding to Riveria, she followed the familia members.

Meanwhile, Riveria left the rear guard to Aiz now that the squad had flipped directions, and she raised the crystal in her hand to her mouth.

"Finn—hook, line, and sinker."

"Good job, Riveria."

The oculus delivered her voice to the supreme commander of the operation. The goal of Riveria's diversionary squad was to catch the creature's attention, lure her out, and draw her as far as possible from Finn and the others. Levis posed the greatest threat to them. With her position known, the biggest source of concern had been cleared up.

"Squads, increase your speed! This will be the decisive point of the operation—push now and don't let up!" echoed the prum's order through the magic item.

After determining Levis's location, every other squad picked up the pace. More precisely, they had been moving in ways that maintained an escape route, but now they discarded thoughts of retreat and devoted themselves to attacking. Bete's squad howled, Gareth's rampaged, Tione's shouted, and the Xenos's roared. Each party began devouring the labyrinth, moving deeper and more fiercely inside.

The operation switched gears.

There was Finn's command, the ability of Aiz's group to be a match for anyone, and Fels's cheat-like magic item that shattered the barriers of space and time. All of them meshed together, allowing the plan to proceed without any hitches.

As one, the scattered adventurers charged forward with a battle cry, almost like a single organism, consuming the giant labyrinth.

OBSESSION
MANIFEST

Гэта казка іншага сям'і.

бяздомная праява

"…" Barca, the descendant of the master architect Daedalus and the effective sovereign of Knossos, held his tongue.

…It's too fast.

He was speaking of the rate at which the enemy was advancing, the number of floors that the adventurers had swept through.

It'd already been half a day since the allied familias had begun their operation—or maybe it would be more accurate to say it had been only half a day.

With *Loki Familia* leading the way, the adventurers raged forward as though a roaring fire, blazing through the labyrinth as they cleared floors. The fastest squad, the one with animal people, was already on the *eighth*, and every other group had made it to the seventh.

In all honesty, it was unimaginable. He might have been able to believe their feat if this had been in the Dungeon—explored to death and thoroughly mapped. But they were in Knossos, an unknown area to *Loki Familia*. And yet.

When Levis approached the Sword Princess's party…all the other groups suddenly started moving differently. *Even the monsters on the lowest floors.*

There was no way for Barca to know that this was thanks to the magic items provided by Fels. The power to precisely convey information between distant locations was an enormous help for strategic purposes. For Braver to read the subtle changes on the battlefields and give precise orders to each squad in real time was a blow more powerful than any multitude of weapons. It would not be an exaggeration to say that the oculi were the final key to clearing Knossos.

The scenes playing out on the watery screen attested to the extent of the threat posed by these items.

They had lost count of the plants that had been destroyed. The production of new monsters could no longer keep up. The violas were being exterminated by teams of adventurers, and the vargs were being annihilated by the vanguards' unrestrained charges. The remnants of the Evils were putting up a fight, but they could not hold out, causing a series of meaningless suicide bombs to go off everywhere.

Using all the information that they gleaned from the two excursions into Knossos before to their full extent, huh…?

Loki Familia was using everything in their arsenal of knowledge as a foundation for their attacks: from the first battle where they withdrew after sustaining casualties and the second attack where they managed to take Barca and the others by surprise. All of it.

While the tempestuous battle of first-tier adventurers had unfolded, the other familia members had made note of the routes taken, which set the course for this assault by illuminating the demons' lair.

They'd managed to weaponize their rage at the loss of their comrades and their knowledge as adventurers, and they were looking to crush Knossos.

"I guess the thousand-year history of my ancestors can be overcome…"

He was being shown the difference between the Dungeon, which defied even the gods' calculations, and Knossos, which was created by mortal hands.

Built by humans, it would inevitably produce some sort of regularity, some sort of order. The stone paving, the routes, the position of the doors—all had a definite intention behind them. And if the creator was a person and not a god, it could not be perfect. Barca felt like he had a small taste of the anguish that Daedalus had felt while pursuing the perfect chaos.

Loki Familia had closed in on that pattern during their previous two encounters with the labyrinth, boldly adapting to it while building up countermeasures.

Why should those who challenged the depths of the Dungeon, which exceeded fifty floors, find an eighteen-floor man-made area difficult?

Barca shuddered as the scenes reflected on the screen continued to disappear, a measure of the speed with which *Loki Familia* was advancing, destroying all the observational eyes as they went. In a detached way, he idly wondered if this was how rulers felt right before their castles fell.

"They're pressing onto the eighth floor now!"

"What do we do?! What do we do now?!"

"At this rate, there's no choice but for the leaders to go…!"

"…" Barca was silent in thought as he glanced around the labyrinth master's room at the leaders yowling like rabid animals.

The prided stronghold of the Evils was being cleared out. There were those among the lawless villains who already recognized what was happening, starting to try to escape the labyrinth. It was still too early to draw a conclusion, but at this rate, if they did not play the ace up their sleeve and release the spirits, Knossos would fall.

Barca's goal was not to join the God of Death's believers in their fate. He would do whatever it took for the sake of his dearest wish. In which case, he was left with a certain option—

"Barca, dear."

All of a sudden, Thanatos snaked his arm around Barca's shoulders. He had silently walked up behind him at some point.

"Are you thinking of *selling* information on Knossos and siding with *Loki Familia*?"

"…"

"Would you betray us…for the sake of protecting Knossos?" A smile loomed on the face beside him. The slender arm wrapped around his shoulders was serpentine.

The god had seen through Barca's inner plan.

Barca wanted to finally fulfill Daedalus's greatest wish: the completion of Knossos. If he could accomplish that, then there was no need for him to fixate on the Evils. He had been one of Thanatos's followers until now, but that was only because it had been convenient for the purposes of expanding Knossos. Barca had no loyalty. All he had was an ancestral delusion that had been passed down for a thousand years.

It was to the point that he was willing to surrender and hand over their desired information if *Loki Familia*, who was allied behind the scenes with the Guild, was trying to eradicate all those who were looking to destroy the city.

"But you see, even if you sold us out, while it would let you live… I can't imagine the Guild…that Ouranos…would allow any further expansion of Knossos. No way."

"…"

"Because any area connecting to the Dungeon would be an obstacle to the peace in the city," Thanatos continued, etching his dark warning into Barca's heart, as if conferring on him a god's divine revelation.

And his words found their mark.

Even if Knossos avoided destruction, no further construction would take place.

If there was another slipup, as with the Xenos incident, the monsters would be able to advance aboveground, and there was no way the Guild would allow any area connecting to the Dungeon to exist.

Barca glanced at the god who made no effort to look at him. The God of Death, androgynous and degenerate, continued to smile—in either scorn or affection for a foolish child. Thanatos slowly turned away from the scenes displayed on the screen to meet Barca's gaze.

"Your desire can only be realized on our side. You knew that."

"…"

"And besides, you aren't an elf. Seeing Knossos to its completion will be impossible for you. You said so yourself. Or could it be that greed is rearing its ugly head?"

"…"

"If it can't be accomplished by your hand, then…let's try to remove as many hinderances for the sake of the next generation. By doing *whatever it takes*."

There was a long silence. The words whispered in Barca's ear were the simple truth.

"…Yes, I know."

In the reflection of the god's eyes, Barca saw himself nodding back expressionlessly. As Thanatos pushed Barca to throw in his lot with them, his eyes arched like a taut bow before he unwound the arm snaked around Barca's shoulders, allowing him to walk out of the room.

"Baaaaarca. Is there anything you need help with?"

"Nothing. If I'm not here, you won't be able to control the doors. I leave the commands to you," Barca responded emotionlessly to the mirthful voice calling out behind him. His gait took on the quality of a wandering soul, causing the frantic familia members to stop and fearfully yield the way to him.

Barca had entirely understood Thanatos's divine will and recognized what was being asked of him. And if Barca, who held the sovereign power over Knossos, was going to leave the labyrinth master's room, where they operated the doors, then it could be for no other purpose than to stop the invaders—*no matter the means or what it took.*

"..."

He walked down a dark hall. His footsteps echoed in the ears of the man with the vacant expression. The inky blackness of the labyrinth ravished his thoughts, exposing his internal hesitation like never before.

—Barca Perdix had *no memory* of ever being attached to something.

In other words, though the years took their toll on his body, he was no different than an infant.

He had never gone aboveground. He had never been exposed to the light of the sun. He did not have normal morals or relations with gods or other people. He knew nothing of love or friendship, ideals or logic.

That was why he lacked emotions and always projected a blank expression.

That was the reason why he was not cognizant of morals, even now that he was aware of them intellectually.

Because of that, Barca could not totally grasp the boundary between self-awareness and the lack of it. Not that he needed that distinction to begin with. In fact, in order to fulfill Daedalus's thousand-year delusion to complete Knossos, this excess functionality was something that needed to be stripped away.

Why...am I replaying the moment I became who I am now...?

It was a scene that Barca could see in a dreamish, illusionary state. The memory of his origin always began with the sound of water.

The water roared, breaking. Barca had been born into this world in the dark labyrinth, bloody body coming out from the womb of the person he called his mother.

With his first wail, the new life was thrust before an open book: Daedalus's Notebook. The blueprints to Knossos were inscribed in it.

"_____"

The baby ceased his sobs, frozen in place with his left eye snapped open wide.

Even though it could not fully observe its surroundings, this eye, inscribed with the symbol *D*, could see that notebook.

"Burn it into that eye! From now on, you will inherit Daedalus's wish! You shall become the next Perdix!"

Perdix. The next manifestation of their ancestor.

The elderly man with the title of Father had wept tears of blood from his veiny eyes, spittle flying from his black-stained teeth, bellowing. His face was etched with obsession as he shouted those words at the living being who hadn't yet been given the name Barca. While the woman suffered, the father gazed at the child with eyes of hatred and emptiness.

Of course, Barca was not troubled by it.

Barca had been *cursed* moments after his birth. His destiny had been swindled from him by that damn notebook. By the fate of his lineage, an innocent infant had turned into a prisoner of Daedalus in the first minute of his life.

There's no mistake—not now or in the future.

From that point on, he had continued as a prisoner in service of the labyrinth: chipping away at the stone face even as his nails tore off. Continuing to expand the labyrinth until he was on the brink of starving to death. Capturing women and forcibly breeding with them.

When those of his family who could not bear the destiny carried by the descendants of Daedalus killed themselves, he carved out their eyes to create new keys.

He was inorganic, beastly, without even the minimal requirement that made a human being. And Barca devoted all his activity to Knossos. In the course of that, exchanging a pledge with a god to receive a Blessing was a natural result.

"—*You have a monster in your heart, Barca.*

"—*A monster: cruel, unsightly, and pure.*"

When he became a follower of the God of Death, Thanatos had said that of him.

Barca thought nothing of it.

Out of necessity, he'd developed the ability Enigma. Out of necessity, he'd become a hexer, forged those repulsive cursed weapons, mass-produced them. Out of necessity, he'd slaughtered people and monsters.

All for the sake of Daedalus's desperate wish.

And yet…I keep replaying the past…replaying Dix's face.

Dix Perdix had been born later from the same womb as Barca, shown the notebook after establishing his own self, and suffered. Barca could not fathom his anguish. Obviously. He had not been equipped with the functions of sympathy or conjecture. But he viewed Dix as a menace for despising Knossos and hindering the completion of their greatest wish from time to time. How he loathed this obstacle.

Dix must have felt similarly toward Barca, who had become nothing more than a function for the purpose of expanding the labyrinth. The only reason they did not try to kill each other was for a mutual benefit. Ironically, that was their one and only fraternal feeling.

What's this sensation?…Well, no matter.

Barca had no faith—no free will. He did not even have the capacity to wonder whether he was a puppet controlled by his blood and a notebook. There was his compulsive obsession, and that was it.

"..."

His sickly white skin was illuminated by the blue light from the magic-stone lamps set in the wall. Wandering down the passage like a lost soul, he approached a hidden room of his own creation, gripping a black notebook in his hand.

Daedalus's Notebook.

He had retrieved the blueprint to Knossos without any strong emotions after Dix had been ruthlessly killed. After silently examining it, he pushed another item in a bag into his belt and hurried to where he was heading.

He arrived at a circular room, narrower than the labyrinth master's room but of a substantial size. The ceiling was high and expansive like an auditorium. There were four entrances. As with the labyrinth master's room, there was a pedestal in the center, which contained a large crimson orb that only descendants of Daedalus could operate.

"Dix...For it to come down to this. For me to rely on your resentment," Barca muttered, murmuring the name of the deceased.

Before his eyes was a maneuvering mechanism. It was the same one that controlled the orichalcum doors, but this one would release the support pillars of the designated floor. The result was a total cave-in. After understanding Thanatos's divine will, Barca was going to use it to collapse an entire floor to crush *Loki Familia*.

It was obviously not a functionality that was recorded in Daedalus's Notebook, for none other than Dix had created that mechanism. His brother from a different father who had resented the notebook, cursed his fate, hated Knossos itself—the man whom Barca did not consider family. As his final rebellion against their ancestor, he had left this behind.

Dix longed to be freed from his cursed blood and dreamed of destroying Knossos itself to achieve his goal.

Barca stood before the destruction mechanism as those meaningless thoughts crossed his mind.

He palmed the notebook in his hands. Thumbing through the

pages, he arrived at the operation instructions that Dix had scribbled in the margins.

Barca turned the crimson orb to the left a half spin and then two full rotations to the right. Finally, he pressed it, silently imagining the destruction. He dictated the collapse to happen on the eighth floor—the area that *Loki Familia*'s allied forces were advancing through. With this, he would be able to eradicate the invaders.

"…"

After pressing the orb disinterestedly, Barca hesitated for a moment.

Even if it was just a single floor on a delusion passed down for a thousand years, its collapse would cause major damage to Knossos. If he did it, the labyrinth's completion would recede beyond his life span, ensuring he would never be able to see through his ancestor's wish.

Though he knew that he would never see the fruition of that obsession, there was a tiny bit of ego that had clung to that distant possibility.

This was the one and only emotion of the man who had never seen the light of day, who was a degenerate, who was sickly white, who did not have the ability to be excited by his emotions. This was his desire and wish. He was conflicted by that lingering attachment.

Ironically, that almost-human ego drew the fateful line between success and failure.

Wrenching open his lips, he started to chant, "*Destructi—*

"——Gh?!"

Shling! A sharp sound rang out in the room, which should have been empty. A beat too late, he heeded the warnings of his sixth sense and bent backward.

A moment later, something cut through the wind, whizzing through the air, drawing a line across Barca's neck. Blood sprayed.

"Guh…?!"

Somehow managing to barely *dodge* it, Barca kicked the ground, trying to retreat in his wobbly state. Daedalus's Notebook slipped from his hand to the ground. Barca could pick up a voice as his blood spurted out, staining his body and the floor.

"—Missed, huh?"

Before his wide crimson eyes, the base of the pedestal started to shimmer. A beautiful woman appeared from thin air, holding a black helmet in her left hand, speaking in a dignified voice.

"...Perseus?!"

A billowing white cloak. Aqua hair paired with silver glasses. Occupying the space before him was the human Asfi Al Andromeda.

"Barca Perdix, if I'm not mistaken. And according to Ikelos, the half brother of Dix Perdix, a descendant of Daedalus...and one of the leaders of the Evils, who killed our comrades."

With a flick, the bloody shortsword in Asfi's right hand whistled through the air. At that signal, several other adventurers materialized from the empty space behind her.

"...Hermes Familia."

A chienthrope thief, a prum mage, a war tiger vanguard. All told, a group of ten people appeared, causing an unusual disturbance in Barca's empty heart. Pressing his hand against his bleeding neck, he felt his parched tongue get caught in place as he tried to say, "Impossible."

"Could you possibly have...a magic item to become invisible?"

Every one of them was holding the same black helmet. From the fact that they appeared by taking off the helmet, he could deduce that they must have been magic items of Perseus's design. They had become invisible, silently encroaching in an attempt to slit Barca's throat.

"But how did you get here...? You shouldn't have been able to find this room without anything short of a miracle, even if you searched the floors high and low..."

He'd managed to process the fact that they'd suddenly appeared before him, but he couldn't help asking this question.

This room was one of the Evils' most important locations in Knossos, along with the labyrinth master's room. Naturally, it was in one of the most complex and deep areas of the labyrinth. It was not a location that could be found by haphazardly stumbling upon it.

"Simple. We caught a person and asked," Asfi offered matter-of-factly, unlike Barca's confused blubbering.

Behind her, the war tiger adventurer tossed a captured person down: one of Thanatos's robed followers. Pulling back the hood revealed a face that Barca recognized. He was someone who served as a commander among the Evils' Remnants, frequently moving around in areas proximal to Thanatos.

"He was prepared to blow himself up, but...when someone invisibly approaches from behind, it leaves no time to execute."

"...!"

"After that, we used an item to have him answer our questions truthfully."

Tossed callously on the ground was a short needle almost resembling an assassin's blade. It must have been another one of Perseus's magic items. They had interrogated him, just like they said, finding out the bases and important locations in Knossos—and securing the location of Thanatos and Barca.

The eyes of the leader lying on the floor were cloudy, rolled back, and twitching.

"...All to find Thanatos and me...?"

"And this notebook, too."

"!"

"To capture the central figures in the organization and steal the blueprints to Knossos. With those in hand, Finn Deimne's original plan for a short, decisive battle can be brought to action."

Bending down, Asfi plucked Daedalus's Notebook from the floor. Because Finn had found out about its existence from Ikelos during the battle on Daedalus Street, he had prioritized getting their hands on the blueprint that spelled out the construction of Knossos. With it, it would eliminate the need to waste any more time mapping the place. It was an imperative of similar value to capturing the critical figures Thanatos and Barca. That notebook was key—the shortcut to success.

"We of *Hermes Familia* were charged with two tasks: to search for clues as to the identity of Enyo...and to concurrently find this notebook."

It wouldn't be wrong to claim that *Loki Familia*'s advance was for the purpose of acquiring that notebook. The left eye inscribed with a *D* opened wide as Barca was struck by a premonition that traveled through his body almost like a shiver.

"You mean…from the very start…?"

"Yes, everything has gone *exactly* according to Braver's plan." Passing the notebook over to the thief, Asfi confirmed his suspicions. "You could say that all the encroaching advances until now acted as our cover to prevent you from noticing our detached force."

Barca's thoughts ran wild as he tried to grasp the situation upon hearing that shocking reality.

Finn had used not just his own squad but all his forces as a diversion. The overabundance of recruited mappers, the invasion by five separate squads, the human-wave tactics—all their efforts to clear Knossos were for the sake of deceiving Barca's side. While they were focused on the advance tearing through the labyrinth, *Hermes Familia* had used the magic item Hades Head to become invisible and move around in secret—allowing them to capture the man on the floor and gather information about the key locations in Knossos.

"This large-scale operation was a trap…? Impossible…"

No one would have believed that *Loki Familia*'s entire forces were being used as a diversion. In truth, the Evils' side had their hands full trying to grind the adventurers' advances to a halt. No one noticed that *Hermes Familia* had suddenly disappeared somewhere along the way—not even Barca, who had been tirelessly observing the battle from the labyrinth master's room.

This was when Barca had a realization.

Finn hadn't been directing the others to blind all the labyrinth's eyes to keep Barca and the others from watching their every move. It had been in preparation for stopping them from noticing the abrupt disappearance of *Hermes Familia*.

Dionysus Familia bolstered numbers, *Loki Familia* offered battle teams, and *Hermes Familia* had a detached force specializing in investigative and secret operations. Finn Deimne had devised a plan that happened to bring together all three of the familias in an alliance to outwit the Evils.

"Not without roadblocks. I mean, our handy helper went off somewhere, and it was super hard to find one of the leaders who knew the path. It took suuuuch a long time..."

"Silence, Lulune...Well, I guess it was fortuitous that you happened to be here with the notebook, but that was simply chance."

Asfi shrugged as the chienthrope thief flipped through the notebook, running her eyes over the pages with an ungodly speed. Behind her, the other members of the familia destroyed the pedestal and destruction device installed on it. Barca was unable to stop them, barely able to open his mouth, pleading for an answer to the final question that gnawed at him.

"What about the key...? Including the single group of monsters, *Loki Familia* has five different squads in operation. Even if you were able to get Ishtar's key, there should only have been five..." he pressed, trying to deny the reality staring him in the face.

There were the keys taken from *Ikelos Familia* and stolen by *Loki Familia* during the Xenos incident and the one that Ishtar had in her possession before she was sent back. Meaning the Knossos forces had lost only five keys.

But by the movements of Finn's battle forces, there should have been no way for Asfi's group to move freely about the inside of Knossos.

Asfi pushed up her silver glasses before speaking to the bloodstained heir of Daedalus.

"I *created* it."

"____"

Her voice echoed through the room.

Time stood still. He did not actually comprehend the meaning of the words at first.

"It's not like we were kicking our feet back during the ten days before the operation. Braver had me examine one of the real keys, and we investigated how the orichalcum gates worked with it...and then *created a new one*."

She held up a metallic orb made out of mythril. There was a red orb in the center with a mesh of red lines that had the appearance of a spiderweb engraved in it instead of the *D* symbol.

"With petals from blood-licorice plants, crimson crystals, the compound eye of a deformis spider, and the tears of a moris…it was possible to replicate your family's eye with items from the Dungeon."

Based on the information that her patron god had gotten from Ikelos, Asfi knew that the eyes of Daedalus's descendants were used to make the keys, which allowed her to create a magic item with the same properties as the Daedalus Orb. Of course, Perseus wasn't omnipotent. And it would have been impossible to create this key from scratch without hints.

But it was a different story if she could directly examine a key that *Loki Familia* had stolen and painstakingly pore over it.

The cursed blood of Daedalus's descendants—the eye inscribed with a *D*—radiated a special kind of magic that activated the gates to open and close. Upon noticing that, Asfi analyzed the frequency of its magic after significant trial and error and then combined various ingredients from the Dungeon to imitate it. Pouring in all her knowledge, skill, and Enigma ability, she had managed to re-create a key to Knossos.

"With only ten days, one was my limit, but…that is sufficient."

The woman called a peerless item maker lived up to her reputation. Barca was finally at a loss for words.

"I don't believe I'm particularly prideful, but…I guess I got inspired when shown an irregular magic item. As an item maker myself, I didn't want to lose."

Asfi cast a sidelong glance at the oculus in Lulune's hand. The very existence of this magic item that made advanced communication possible inside the Dungeon across different floors—and the existence of its creator, Fels—had provoked Perseus's professional pride.

"We've got the notebook! I've got a grasp on all the routes!"

And as if to demonstrate the power of that item, Lulune held an oculus to her mouth and shouted. With the notebook in one hand, the thief revealed the locations of the key facilities, spreading Knossos's hidden knowledge in one fell swoop.

"The enemy's base is on...the ninth floor!"

"The demi-spirit is on the tenth floor! With open areas where a floor boss could run wild! Braver, give us your orders!"

Finn clenched his fist as Lulune's voice called out from the oculus in his hand.

"Press in on the enemy's base first! Leave the demi-spirit for now!—To the ninth floor!"

""Yes, sir!"" Tione and the rest responded in unison to his command.

Cutting through the wall of monsters in their way, they lunged forward as if a wild animal hunting down its prey.

"What floor are you on? Tell me about your surroundings, and I'll try to figure out your location and guide you along!"

"'Bout damn time!"

The oculus was conveying the information to Gareth's squad, too. After they cheered over this moment, which they had been waiting for since Finn explained the strategy, Gareth rattled off to Lulune the details of the surrounding area that their group had mapped.

"Miss Filvis!"

"Yes! Aura, spread the word to Enol and the others!"

"I know!"

The morale of the elven girls shot through the roof. Even though she barked back at Filvis for calling out to her, Aura spread the news, and *Dionysus Familia* broke out in a roar of excitement.

"How many entrances are there? And where are they?! Gimme all the deets!" Bete howled.

"I—I got it! There are three! In the north, southeast, and southwest!" a panicked voice shot back in response.

The team of animal people advancing to Knossos's ninth floor picked up speed again.

"Secure all the passages between the Dungeon and the ninth floor! We can't let Thanatos get away! Tell the group behind us! We're splitting up! Bete and I are taking one team, and Raul will take the other!" The second-in-command, Anakity, shot off orders, hammering out their squad's next movements.

Once they had finished off the enemies, the stairway had become a safe zone, where she placed *Dionysus Familia* members to seal off any routes of escape to the other floors. *Loki Familia* was exterminating all the monsters while taking control of the only three ways out of the ninth floor.

Suddenly, they had closed the net around the ninth floor and the enemy's base.

All according to Braver's plan.

"Check. We got them cornered on one side of the board now."

"And what if they have something up their sleeve to turn things around?"

"Well, maybe if this labyrinth went *BOOM* and transformed into a giant fighter...or the spirits ran wild. But those are the only options," added Loki, cracking jokes with Dionysus as the enemy soldiers cried out in despair and scattered before them.

But her eyes narrowed.

"—They got me."

Finally, Thanatos closed his eyes and leaned back in the labyrinth master's room, where he'd been watching over their movements, facing the ceiling, as if admitting defeat.

"Can you hear that? Can you hear the footsteps of destruction closing in around you?"

Stomping echoed all through the labyrinth, as though the march of a military force. Barca was dumbstruck as it reached his ears. While Lulune was sending out a never-ending stream of instructions through the various oculi in her possession, Asfi coldheartedly informed him of the battle's outcome.

Barca did not move. He was no longer able to react in the blink of an eye to the strategy unfolding before him. The blood dripping from his neck created a pool on the floor, plinking against the stone tiles as if a clock ticking down to the end.

"…—!"

From one of the entrances connecting to the rest of Knossos, *Loki Familia* adventurers appeared: the squad led by Finn, including Tiona and Tione, along with Amid and the other healers from *Dian Cecht Familia*. Their main fighting force.

It was a group of ten—less than when they'd entered Knossos, because they had dispersed their forces to gain full control of the ninth floor. However, with Tiona and the rest, their collective strength was more than sufficient. There were far too many of them for Barca to take on his own.

Everything that had happened in their absence must have been shared via the oculi. There was no visible surprise on their faces as Finn faced off with Barca, who was unable to even move.

"This is the end, Barca Perdix—no, the remnant of the Evils. We shall be taking our revenge…for the murdered members of our familia in the Dungeon," Asfi said as she readied her shortsword.

Barca lowered the hand that pressed against the cut on his throat. With his arms dangling at his sides, a sense of resignation filled his eyes, which were hidden behind his white hair.

"…This is where I meet my end, huh?"

As he let the blood flow out, he moved his hand to his belt, drawing his hidden shortsword, his cursed weapon.

Amid's eyes narrowed when she saw the pitch-black blade with a tip that was far more sinister than any of the ones held by the regular soldiers of the Remnants. The other adventurers were on guard and readied themselves.

In the face of them, Barca raised his cursed weapon.

"?!"

And he stabbed that cursed blade into *his own body*.

"Wh—?!"

"I-into himself?!"

"Wh—…? Suicide?!"

He did not stop there. He unsheathed another cursed shortsword and gored himself again. Over and over and over.

Alongside Tione, Tiona, and Asfi, everyone was shocked at the sight. Even Finn and the healer Amid were unable to peel their eyes away in disbelief.

He punctured his stomach, shoulder, legs, arms. He was avoiding his vitals, but it was clear this would be lethal. After sustaining these curses, he coughed up tarry blood.

"As you said…it's our loss. The Evils will be crushed here," Barca announced in an empty voice, plastered in blood, as his death approached.

Loki Familia and *Hermes Familia* were taken aback by his ominous figure as the man struggled to breathe. The eye with an inscribed *D* opened wide.

"But—Knossos shall not die."

In the next instant, he took something out of the bag hanging from his belt: a green jewel.

"Wh—…? The fetus of a crystal orb?!" Asfi shouted in surprise.

The chienthrope Lulune, the prum Merrill, and the war tiger Falgar were taken aback. It was a seed of the corrupted spirit—the one seen by their fallen comrades in the twenty-fourth-floor pantry, the one that parasitically fed on monsters and turned into its powerful female form before evolving into a demi-spirit.

Barca took out a crystal orb that was far bigger than the one Asfi remembered, pulsing with a thick, veiny thing that was entwined on its surface. The fetus inside it opened its bloodshot eyes, staring down the adventurers.

"The six seeds have already been released. This is an *extra*. Ironically, it's the same crystal orb that *Hermes Familia* offered their blood to on the twenty-fourth floor," Barca choked out, hacking up blood.

He looked intently at *Hermes Familia*, speaking as if it was all fated to be. As they reacted to the "twenty-fourth floor" in rage, he roared back—with *even greater fury*.

"Our glorious dream shall not be crushed! Our obsession shall not come to an end! In order to complete the chaos as dreamed by our ancestor, I will bring as many of you with me as I can!"

That was the final cry of the human known as Barca—the man who had never achieved self-awareness, who had always been unclear on the line between self and other. He established a definite selfhood for the first time, raising a wail, full-throated and clear.

A newborn's first cry.

It established a direct connection between him and his lineage's undying curse.

—*It can't be.* Asfi realized what he was about to do but was too late.

Barca raised the crystal orb and pressed it into his own chest.

"Gu—geeeh—gaaaaaaaaaaaaaaaaaaaaaaaaaaaaaaaaaaah?!"

"—*Aaaaaaaaaaaaaaaaaah!*"

The man's howl and the fetus's cry overlapped—in a fusion, not with a monster but with a human.

The fetus of a crystal orb could parasitize more than just monsters. With the possibility that she'd mulled over happening before her very eyes, Asfi's train of thought derailed as she was locked in place.

Veiny tubes of leaves expanded from its fusion site on his chest. The fetus's tentacles ran across his whole body, mercilessly eating away at his flesh, overrunning it, rearranging its composition.

The man's right arm swelled hideously out of shape. His left arm snapped out like a whip, stretching and losing all human form. His legs rotted away as he assumed the shape of a slug. The veiny structures turned pitch-black, as if absorbing all the curses that he had inflicted on himself, causing the fetus to cry out. But the blackened veins kept pulsating, carrying the darkness to the crystal orb on his chest, staining it black as well.

The room filled with the disgusting squelches of flesh blending and cracks of bones breaking as the shape of Barca's body was rearranged with terrifying speed. It was the birth of a powerful being, formed from a body that rivaled an upper-class adventurer—from a body of one who wielded the Enigma ability.

The members of *Loki Familia* and *Hermes Familia* turned pale. The Amazonian twins moaned in disgust, the eyes of the prum hero narrowed, and the jack-of-all-trades pursed her lips.

And faced with a blasphemy of life itself, the holy woman gripped her staff, causing the blood to drain out of her hands.

"Ogoo, ah, ah, ah, ah…ga, ah, ah, ah, ah……aaaaaaaaaaa…!"

As the corrosion reached his mind, his face transformed into that of a monster. As his eyes streamed tears of blood and his right one rolled back, the left one with a *D* tenaciously maintained its form.

His crimson eyes focused, glaring at the enemies standing in front of him. Just before Barca Perdix's sense of self melted away entirely, he entrusted his final resolve to the fetus.

"You will die…here…adventurerrrrrrrrrrrrrrrrs!" he managed to bellow.

No sooner had that escaped from its throat than its body swelled. It had transformed into a giant figure beyond human recognition.

With that, the descendant of Daedalus, the man keeping a monster in his heart, stood against the adventurers, having been reduced to a true monster.

"Ready yourselves!" rang out the order in a speed faster than lightning.

With Finn's call, the familia members shook themselves out of their natural instincts to retreat. They could feel Braver's courage in his voice, managing to overcome their terror and point their weapons at the repulsive monster.

"*Goooooooooooooooooooooooo!*" roared the monster that no longer had the ability to speak, sending shivers through the adventurers.

The being that had once been Barca Perdix had already completed its transformation. Its right arm was enlarged, its left arm an elongated tentacle, and its legs had morphed into a sluglike tail. Its head looked like a collection of insect eggs. While every other part of it had morphed, inducing a visceral disgust, its left eye, inscribed with the letter *D*, remained unchanged and blazed without the light of intelligence. Its cloudy white body had pitch-black veins pulsing all over it, creating a gnarly contrast. It was over five meders tall, on the same scale as a large monster.

That was the result of offering his own body to the crystal orb fetus. If it was to be given a name, it would have to be simple: the Barca Monster. He had chased after that desperate dream too long, going to the point of discarding all human form. It was the manifestation of Daedalus's obsession.

"Ew! Disgusting! Grooooosss! I don't even want to touch it with Urga!"

"Don't be stupid! What are you going to do—punch it with your fist?!"

"I don't want to do that, either!"

Tiona readied her Urga and Tione held out her twin Zolas, not losing sight of their goal even as they shouted back and forth. They were paying the utmost caution when faced with an unknown enemy unlike any they'd fought before.

Just when it seemed that the Barca Monster was finally standing still, it suddenly started moving without any notice.

"Incoming!" Asfi warned, just as it unleashed an attack with its left arm.

The white tentacle covered with black veins swung down from above, crashing into the center of the room, causing the two familias to rush to either side. Lulune had been exchanging reports using the oculi throughout all of it and lost her cool as she scrambled. The vanguards rushed in as the room started to quake.

"Aaaaaaaaaaaaaaah!" erupted a baritone howl as the Barca Monster swung its enlarged right arm at them.

The limb was shaped like a gourd, but the force behind it was brutal. It sent a spiderweb of cracks to break through the ground, shattering the stone flooring and causing even those who boasted high dexterity to stumble. It used that opportunity to start flailing its left tentacle at random, pushing them back away from it.

"Guh...?!"

"Falgar! Thane! Leave the vanguard to *Loki Familia*! We'll focus on supporting them with Merrill!"

As the war tiger and elf were repelled, Asfi took out three Burst Oils and threw them. Three crimson explosions flared. The damage was minor, but it created an opening. With the help of the other familia, Tione and Tiona closed in through the smoke of the explosion, hounding it like wild animals.

"Its movements are sluggish! Tiona, *knock it back*!"

"Got it!"

Taking notice that the fused legs of the enemy weren't agile, Tiona took the lead. As she closed in, she swung Urga up, attempting to slice into its right arm.

"—Gh?!"

An audible *thud* echoed through the room. The full force of her charge had been stopped. The herculean strength pressing back against her caused Tiona's eyes to snap open in surprise, but she was all smiles again.

"Gareth iiiiiiis...even stronger...than thiiiiiis...!"

With a sharp pivot of her waist, she knocked it away, serving it as ordered. Tione immediately cut in as the Barca Monster stumbled back, wobbling off-balance as its giant right arm went whizzing past its head.

"Rot in hell!"

The sisters' teamwork would secure them an instantaneous win.

"!!"

But feeling an ache in his thumb, Finn was the first to react. "Tione and Tiona, get away!"

""?!""

They doubted their ears when they heard his order, but they obeyed him immediately as a rule. And a split second after they beat a hasty retreat, the black veins stretched around the monster's body bulged with an audible creak.

"_____"

All the adventurers in the room, those who had crossed through a multitude of situations with their lives on the line, felt a shiver go down their spines. In the next instant, its veins burst, unleashing an immense shower of blood.

"Whaaaaaat?!"

"Gah?!"

Tiona and Tione were the closest to it and swung their weapons, evading it as first-tier adventurers, but the others in the vanguard fell prey to the attack.

"Aaaaaaaaaaaaaaaaaaaaaaaaaaaaaagh?!" shrieked those in the perimeter who'd been pelted by the black rain.

Their skin turned a revolting jet the instant they made contact with the droplets, and as blood spurted out of their eyes, noses, and mouths, they writhed in agony. Regardless of whether they were members of *Loki Familia* or *Hermes Familia*, they collapsed to the ground and rolled around in pain. Moans of broken spirits permeated the room.

It had all happened in the blink of an eye, leaving everyone rigid with shock.

"Poison?! No...it can't be...A curse?!"

Asfi's eyes opened wide in disbelief at this indescribable scene. Even those with Status abilities that resisted afflictions suffered the same symptoms. It was indiscriminate. The *Loki Familia* members were taken aback, then started using the anti-curse medicine on those who were afflicted.

"Gaaaaaaaargh...?!"

"I-it isn't working?! The anti-curse medicine won't break them free?!"

They kept coughing up blood, cries piercing through the ears of everyone in the room. Tiona, Tione, and Finn were motionless. Amid, standing by at the back, caught her breath.

It was an extremely powerful curse. The blood splattered the floor, giving off a black smoke. Filling the room with its toxic miasma, the Barca Monster started spraying its black blood again.

The attack gave rise to a chain of screams from the vanguard.

Its unnatural convulsions continued as the adventurers dragged the comrades at death's door away from the black rain. But the spray from the enemy was not something they could easily avoid while holding those who were immobile. Its ceaseless pelts caused many more people to collapse. The perimeter around the monster crumbled in an instant.

"Dia Frater!" Amid activated her magic with a high-speed chant.

A pure white light poured down on those who had collapsed, granting them protection. The bloody adventurers coughed as their convulsions died down. While their wounds healed, they looked as though they'd suddenly woken up from a bad dream.

"A-Amid's magic can heal it!"

"But that means…!"

In contrast to the relief in Tiona's voice, Tione sounded uneasy.

Its curse could be healed only by the city's greatest healer. In other words, it was effectively a one-hit kill. If Amid had not been there, they would not have been able to maintain their battle lines. Losing her would guarantee defeat.

"Protect Amid!" Finn issued an immediate order.

The frontline tanks responded with all their strength, creating a series of walls to cover the healer from *Dian Cecht Familia*. What was to come was hell on earth.

"Uh…Waaaaaaaaah?!"

The scattershot of the curse sowed suffering in all directions. Regardless of vanguard or rear guard, its range could reach as far as the walls in any direction. Those who were slow to evade were inflicted with an otherworldly level of pain. The mages trying to cast spells faced a particularly tragic end. They could not move immediately because they were chanting, leading to them becoming drenched in the revolting curse.

"Gaaaaaaaaaah?!"

"Merrill!" screamed the war tiger, covering *Hermes Familia*'s prum mage in the midst of preparing a barrage with a large shield.

"The recovery isn't fast enough…! Captain Finn, *my healing power can't keep up!*"

For the first time, Amid looked anxious as she held her staff and cast her magic.

If anyone could have seen the battle from the outside, they would not have believed their eyes. A monster and holy woman—the boundary between light and dark, cursing and healing—were ruthlessly butting heads with a miasmic damnation and a storm of white radiance. Their two domains clashed for supremacy, splitting the battlefield in two.

Those healed by Amid were soon being eaten away at by the curse again. The party members were in a state of confusion at the world of half destruction that ruled over the battlefield as an unending loop of regeneration and devastation continued. If even one thing went wrong, the adventurers' formation would collapse entirely in the blink of an eye.

"Barca Perdix…! Did he know this would happen when he stabbed himself?!" Asfi groaned as she protected her skin with her white mantle.

There was a reason why he had stabbed himself with the cursed weapons with such tenacity: to have the crystal orb fetus parasitize a body that had stored up curses, giving rise to a monster with an ability that it should have had no way of developing.

Namely, a monster that could weaponize curses.

Asfi's face tightened at that horrifying concept.

In the midst of the adventurers scrambling to escape, Lulune was balancing the notebook and a handful of oculi as she yelled out, "A-Asfi?! At this rate, shouldn't we get some other—?"

"—Absolutely not!" Finn snapped, cutting off her desperate plea.

Lulune and *Hermes Familia*, plus Amid and the healers and the rest of *Loki Familia*, were all shocked by his bark as he spun his spear like a windmill to protect his comrades.

"If Amid is the only one who can heal this, it won't matter if we bring more squads into the fight! All it will do is increase the casualties!"

"—...?!"

It would be meaningless to call for backup. As Lulune and several others despaired, Finn continued, "What was the goal of this operation?! Don't forget! We cannot fail to capture their ringleaders! We can't allow all our forces to be concentrated in one place!"

"!!"

"Gareth's squad is closing in on Thanatos! Meaning we—alone—must defeat this enemy!"

His pronouncement was resonant and unwavering as he spoke strategically rather than tactically. His voice was enough to help them recover their morale, even though they were between a rock and a hard place.

Calculating that the enemy's attack was letting up for a second, Finn held his golden Fortia Spear in one hand, raising aloft the weapon whose very name was the embodiment of courage.

"Let's charge!"

It wasn't a call for them to advance on their own, but he'd added that they would *all* rush forward. Meaning Finn himself would be joining the front lines. It was a bombastic exhortation as he set aside his role as commander and stood at the very front, showing them the way to clear a path.

"Take up your shields! Forget about evasion! Show your courage and stop its attacks head-on! This is when you prove yourself as an adventurer!"

Finn had been defeated by this curse once. He had been unable to recover after an assault by none other than Levis. But this was not about trying to redeem himself, not about restoring his honor, not about earning vindication. What he displayed was only his bravery.

As Finn sprinted without holding a shield, he cut into the Barca Monster. He lurched himself into the rain, not shrinking back from the curse that had almost gotten him once before. He displayed his small, powerful, reliable back to the adventurers who were desperately recoiling in the face of the curse.

"G-get up! Get uuuuuup!"

"Follow the captaiiiiiiiiiiiiin!"

And the familia members answered his call. His inspiration lit a fire in them, allowing their morale to overcome their fear. Hoisting their shields high, they chased after the prum, reminded that no matter how great the enemy, squaring off against a powerful foe and following the bravery embodied by their small hero was what it meant to be part of *Loki Familia*.

Tiona and Tione raised a battle cry as they led familia members charging in from other directions. Leaving behind the confounded members of *Hermes Familia*, they displayed the pride of the most powerful familia in Orario.

We must break this curse, the adventurers roared.

CHAPTER 6

AND
THEN
THE
GOD
SMILED

Гэта казка іншага сям'і.

І Бог засмяяўся

"Elfie, hurry up!"

"I'm sorry, Miss Aliciaaaaa!"

Alicia looked back as Lefiya's roommate, Elfie, desperately tried to keep up as they rushed through the passages.

On the ninth floor of Knossos.

Their group had originally been part of Finn's squad but had split off into a smaller group. After the transmission from *Hermes Familia*, Finn had given the order to his squad to branch off, following the footsteps of the other groups. Elfie was racing around the labyrinth with the group under Alicia's command, working to set up a perimeter around the floor. Their group was composed of six people. With the mage Elfie in the mix and led by the Level-4 Alicia, they had enough firepower to move around the floor by themselves. Now that the enemy's strength had been whittled down, that was more than adequate force to make a splash.

Thanks to Lulune's report, they knew that Barca was currently on the battlefront, meaning they no longer needed to fear the enemy opening or closing doors remotely. And with guidance from the thief who had the labyrinth's blueprints, they did not have to worry about losing their way.

They were working hard to finish off the last pockets of enemy resistance.

"____?"

Elfie had been desperately sprinting, in real danger of being left behind by the speedy vanguards, when—*Shrick.* Elfie heard metal scraping against stone.

"What was that...?"

It was the sort of noise that could never happen naturally in the stone-paved labyrinth. But it was trivial enough that she did not even think to shout a warning about a possible trap.

They were in one segment of the passage.

Elfie instinctively stopped in her tracks and glanced around. What caught her eye was the wall diagonally behind her, where there was a small crack in the labyrinth walls, which were supposed to have been constructed from adamantite. That was where the sound was coming from. It was faint, but it kept repeating, low enough that it was drowned out by the ambient sounds of fighting in the distance if she did not listen carefully.

A self-admitted bundle of curiosity, Elfie forgot all about her current situation and approached the crack, drawn to it. Suspicious, or perhaps disturbed, she gulped as she peeked inside.

Peering into the deep, dark void through the crack, she saw what looked like an empty cavern. In that darkness, something was writhing, and in time with its movements, a clanking sound rang out, as though chains were being tugged.

Elfie held her breath. She squinted, as if doubting her sight, focusing—

All of a sudden, a bloodshot eye appeared in front of her.

"—Eraaaaaaaaaaaaaaaaaaaaaaaaaaaaaaaaaaaaaaaaaaaah?!" she screamed oddly, leaping back.

The shadow in the darkness rammed into the cracked wall with a *thud*, seeming to notice her presence. Elfie landed spectacularly on her butt after hopping back in surprise.

"Wh-wh-what was that?! Was that a monster?!"

From her position on the ground, Elfie gripped her chest and readied her rod before her. The eye floated in space, peering out of the crack, while its owner moaned hoarsely in a way that the gods jokingly discussed how zombies were purported to groan. It scraped against the wall as if attempting to break free.

"Elfie, what are you doing?!"

"Miss Aliciaaaaaaaaaaaaaaaaa?! Th-there's something inside this wall!"

"What are you talking about?! We have to deal with the monsters! We're going to get surrounded!"

Elfie's eyes clouded over as Alicia yelled back at her from farther down the passage. Looking ahead, she saw that they were already in the middle of a fight—the monsters were approaching from the same direction that their squad had taken to get there.

"The terrain is bad! We're changing locations and counterattacking! Get a move on and join us!"

"U-understood!" Elfie stood up in a rush, reluctantly leaving behind the crack in the wall.

She trailed after Alicia to the others waiting for her. The eye floating in darkness stared, fixated on her back, as if trying to follow her.

"Prepare yourselves! Incoming!" Riveria shouted as soon as she set foot into the open space.

Loki Familia had spread out in the room on the twelfth floor. A group of heavily armed troops, Level 3 and higher, had been deployed in advance to confront the powerful prey they had lured out. After they had broken into Knossos, they had found an area that fit their requirements, and Riveria had left a dedicated counterattack force there.

The mages readied their staffs, tensing and starting to chant their spells in unison as Aiz in the rear guard leaped into the room. Not a moment later, the figure of a woman with bloodred hair skidded into the space.

"You really ran around, Aria."

"...—!"

Levis's gaze pierced into Aiz, who stopped in the center of the room and turned around. The strongest creature was holding a cursed longsword, looking pessimistic as always. Her gaze was trained only on Aiz, flashing Riveria alone a cursory glance, but she did not look once at the rest of the people spread around the room.

"L-Lady Riveria...!"

"Do not be rash. Aiz and I will hold her back to start," she replied to the elves as they became visibly distraught after spotting the creature, urging them to control themselves.

To deal with Levis, their plan was to place Aiz at the front with Riveria's support while the rest of the squad bombarded her. Riveria kept her eyes fixed on Levis as she shrank the magic circle to a radius of five meders, down from the full range that she needed to keep a lookout for the creature's approach. If the creature and the vanguard ever clashed, her *Rea Laevateinn*'s flames could erupt at a moment's notice.

A wall of warriors with great shields stood in front of the mages who had completed their casts. They all fixed Levis with determined glares, cold sweat forming on their brows. The room took on a charged atmosphere—as if an ammunition dump ready to explode at a moment's notice.

"...?"

Aiz was facing off against Levis, and she furrowed her brow dubiously. Levis stood before her, looking at Aiz with a blank expression. All she was doing was observing her.

She isn't attacking...?

She did not even ready her sword. Not only that, Aiz could not sense a threatening aura. The forces behind Aiz were mystified as she faced the creature who was just standing there. Even Riveria was split between being on guard and trying to figure out what the hell was going on.

"...—?"

Aiz had fought the Warlord to prepare for this moment. She had approached this operation ready to reach a conclusion in her battle with Levis. But their current situation was too unexpected. She did not know what to do. If Levis attacked, she was determined to respond. She was resolved to fight to the end. However, she herself was not able to attack.

Once the battle started, it was clear there would be casualties. If the opponent was going to spend her time doing nothing, then that was the best possible result. For the purposes of Finn seizing control of Knossos and for their own purposes, a stalemate was the ideal scenario.

This was beyond their wildest imagination, but this was also extraordinarily convenient. It should have been exactly what they wanted. But Aiz could not swallow the intense unease she felt, standing face-to-face with the creature who was her archenemy without crossing swords.

"…"

Levis allowed time to pass as she silently watched Aiz, perplexed, as she maintained her stance.

"Cynthia! Halberd!"

"G-got it!" shouted the mage supporter in response to Tione, tearing a large weapon off her backpack.

She handed over the Durandal special, Roland Halberd. Switching to the longer weapon, Tione sliced into the Barca Monster.

"Gaaaaaaaaaaaaaaah!"

The ax made its landing in its swollen right arm, sending blood gushing out. *Ts*king as she dodged the spray of black blood, Tione used her pole weapon's reach to attack and evade at range. With Tione's and Finn's repeated attacks leading the way, the rest of *Loki Familia* resolutely lunged in one after the other with spears and glaives.

"Surround it! Surround it!"

"Mages! Don't stop casting your spells!"

"Don't worry about scorching all of it! Just fall back!"

The hall on the ninth floor had transformed into a grueling battlefield where the fighting was thick with shields to deal with the cursed black rain. Other than Tiona, all the adventurers had switched to pole or ranged shooting weapons, including bows and arrows. The monster was using its hardened right arm to ward them off and knocking away magic with its cursed left tentacle, but the attacks never ceased. *Hermes Familia* might have had less combat power to offer, but they contributed superb support on both offense and defense.

"That even *Loki Familia* would struggle to bring it down…!" Asfi squinted as she looked at the monster that would not fall, withstanding the attacks.

Their enemy was specialized for defense. In exchange for agility, its giant slug of a body was as unmovable as a thousand-year-old tree towering over its surroundings. It endured the adventurers' attacks, throwing countermeasures with its deformed arms. The rain of blood prevented all from getting close, and even when they managed to slip through, they could not land a critical hit from the off-balance stances that they needed to get through the pelts. Even Tiona's Urga could not sever any of its limbs.

The parasitic crystal orb fetus—the blackened sphere that was the enemy's core—sat exposed in the center of its chest, protected by a hardened substance like a budding flower that prevented them from killing it with one blow.

On top of all that, the enemy had the pesky ability of regeneration. The blood vessels all over its body continually burst and re-formed in a speed that surpassed the damage, causing even *Loki Familia*'s adventurers to groan. Tiona, Tione, and Finn all judged that it had a potential even greater than the female form they had fought on the eighteenth floor.

They were in a fortress formation with high defensive capabilities to endure enemy attacks while using its curse to consign to oblivion all who faced it. Even as they shuddered at the monster that would have annihilated them in an instant, they didn't have a means of recovery as they continued to work together and courageously chip away at the enemy's stamina.

"Graaaaaaaaaaaaaagh!"

But there were many casualties. If a single drop of the scattered blood touched someone's skin, a bloodcurdling shriek broke through the fray. Frontline fighters fell, unable to block the rain of blood with their shields. And even those who evaded the cursed droplets started to hemorrhage blood as they kept breathing in its damned miasma. The curse, the unconditional murderous intent, afflicted everyone standing in the room.

If not for the healing white light pushing back against it, it would not even be a fight. When people collapsed, Amid engaged her recovery magic.

"The man who became the monster's host…He was the creator of that repulsive curse…!"

Watching the battlefield from the back, Amid was sure of it. The one reduced to a monster was the same hexer who had created the cursed weapons, the originator of that abominable damnation. She realized that the curse's power was enhanced, as if resonating with Barca Perdix's Status—with his Enigma ability.

In order to complete Knossos, Barca had needed to develop several abilities. All for the sake of that, he had leveled up three times. Harboring an obsession that no normal person could begin to understand, his body was the ideal host for the fetus of the crystal orb, which feasted on it—or overdosed. In fact, it was compatible enough to trigger this bizarre evolution, giving birth to a monster that specialized in killing with curses, something that should never have been possible.

Amid, who wielded the same Enigma ability herself, recognized what was happening. "A tremendous obsession with this labyrinth…Is that the true nature of your curse?"

One of the reasons that Amid had wanted to take part in this operation was because she had learned of the origin of Knossos, of the descendant of Daedalus Barca Perdix: the source of the curse.

She had wondered if perhaps he had been cursed by his lineage—a victim—and if that unbroken bloodline was the origin of the curse. Now that he had become a monster, his body trapped in the web of black veins seemed to prove it.

"—Then we must break the chains of that curse," Amid spoke resolutely as she held her staff. "Marta, Bernadette. Take over the recovery in my stead. Please support the battle lines."

""Y-yes!""

The two healers from *Dian Cecht Familia* who had been waiting behind her joined in for the first time that day. Not because Dea Saint was no longer able to fully maintain the battlefield herself. But because she devoted herself to breaking the chains of the curse rather than healing.

"*Healing droplets, tears of light, eternal sanctuary. Compose a medicinal hymn—three hundred, sixty, and five. The melody of the healer's almanac saves all things.*"

Her clear voice composed a high-speed cast. It was the same spell, but the adventurers recognized that it had more force behind it this time. The Barca Monster seemed to have a premonition and cast a mist of black blood toward Amid.

"Falgar!"

"Haaaaaaaah!"

With the war tiger in the middle, the others blocked it with their shields. With Finn at the front lines and Asfi commanding the middle and back lines, they did not allow any breaks in either their attacks or defense of Amid.

"Come, destruction of evil. The burial of wounds, interment of disease. Curses be gone in the light of vitality."

The Barca Monster divided the battlefield with its tentacle, smashing into the shields, but Falgar gritted his teeth, determined not to create an empty space in their defense.

"In the name of all that is holy—I heal you."

Amid responded to their desperate struggle.

"Dia Frater!" she chanted, unleashing her complete healing magic, the pure white illumination of holy power, toward...the Barca Monster.

"What?!"

"Amid?! What are you thinking trying to heal a monster?!"

Tiona and Tione yelped, vocalizing what everyone on the battlefield was thinking. Upon witnessing the unprecedented act of healing a monster, anyone would have doubted the real motives of this holy woman. In the midst of all that, Finn and Asfi had a different reaction, eyes wide in surprise when they understood exactly what Amid was trying to do.

"———————————————*Gh?!*"

The Barca Monster started suffering. Bathed in the holy light with the potential to heal all—person or monster—it started writhing with an accelerated fervor, twisting its body in pain. As steam rose from its body, the *black color in its veins gradually dissipated.* When Tione gazed in wonder with her comrades, her doubts began to melt away.

"She's dispelling the curse!" Asfi yelled.

"Huh? What? Huh?" Lulune looked back and forth in confusion.

"Dea Saint is dispelling the curse! She isn't healing the monster's body! She aimed only at the curse!"

Amid's *Dia Frater* was the greatest healing spell, capable of healing wounds, restoring stamina, clearing poison, and dispelling curses. It was an extremely useful capability that could be split into three different effects: recovery, poison eradication, and curse removal. It could heal those sobbing over their wounds and extract poison from those suffering its consequences. At her discretion, she could selectively choose to use only one or two of the possible effects of her spell.

It was mainly an ability to limit using up her Mind unnecessarily, but this time, she poured everything into dispelling the curse—into removing the curse that had accumulated in the Barca Monster.

"A healer rendering a monster powerless, huh? Will wonders never cease…!" Finn murmured with a shudder as the flood of holy light dissipated.

Instead of using it on her allies, she had hit the enemy with her magic to clear the curse. That act had surprised everyone, but none could look away from what ensued.

"Be gone, malevolent curse. As a healer…I cannot allow such a thing to exist," Amid said, illuminated by her magic light.

The white magic circle expanded beneath the Barca Monster's feet. While it was to eliminate the curse, the magic power shot up as though a cannon blast assaulting the monster. The torrent of purifying light became a pillar enclosing it.

"Now that you've become who you are, I cannot heal you."

"———————Gh?!"

"It would be arrogant to apologize and profane to grieve you. Now that I've given up on saving you, I'm nothing more than a hypocrite—but at least allow me to kill that curse."

The destruction of the curse. The salvation of his spirit. Freeing him from his damned bonds.

Amid spoke as she looked at the monster, clenching in her left hand the magic wand that aided the efficacy of her magic and thrusting out her right palm. Her platinum hair blew back from the shock waves brought on by the light.

The Barca Monster flailed both arms as if being assaulted by the most excruciating pain, burned by the holy light. The thick veins running across its body burbled and swelled, as if boiling, the black curse fading moment by moment. The very reason it had been reduced to that form was gradually disappearing.

"——Oooooooooooooooooooh!"

As if screaming at her not to screw with it, the Barca Monster rampaged. Almost as though the creature was resisting, it unleashed the full strength of its curse at Amid.

"——————————?!"

It was beyond rain. The surging wave of miasmic energy took on the life of a vengeful spirit that consumed Amid. All the adventurers in its path, all those who had formed a wall to protect her, were washed away by the wave of blood. Even the holy robes protecting her body were starting to burn and turn a festering black.

"Amid!"

A clash of white and black. A battle between holy light and curse with which adventurers could not interfere. Blood seeped out from the corner of her mouth.

Her outstretched hand in all its youthful vitality withered like an old woman's. The cries of Tiona, Tione, and the other adventurers grew distant. Amid was consumed by a swirl of pain unlike any she had ever experienced, but she still refused to stop her magic.

"Dae...da—...lus—...!"

"—Gh!"

As if repeating the curse, its D-inscribed eye became bloodshot and burned with the remnants of its will. Seeing that, the holy woman's eyes flashed radiantly.

"Haaaaaaaaaaaaaaaaaaaaaaaaaaah!" Amid let out a triumphant roar.

The brilliant magic light gathered into a giant pillar of pure white, blasting away the miasma. White particles of light scattered around the room as the pitch-black stain enshrouding the Barca Monster finally disappeared. As if it had lost the armor protecting its body.

""Gh!"" As Amid started to collapse, the two Amazons dashed forward faster than anyone else.

They lunged above the monster's head, determined not to let their friend's efforts go to waste as they swung their massive weapons.

"Uraaaaaaaaaaaaaaaagh!"

"Here I gooooooooooooooooooooooo!"

Tione's halberd and Tiona's Urga came crashing down. Their twin attacks severed its arms. Losing its balance, the giant body began to pitch forward.

"—Hah!"

And finally, Finn sprinted head-on. His golden Fortia Spear at the ready, he thrust it toward the monster with tremendous force and speed.

"!!"

But just as the golden spear's tip was about to pierce the monster's head, he stopped short.

"Captain?!" Tione shouted, bewildered that he had stopped right before delivering the final blow. She was about to ask why he had wasted the golden opportunity.

"—It's dead."

"Huh?"

"It's already over," Finn murmured as he gradually lowered his spear.

Tiona and the others stopped moving. Even those suffering from the curse and struggling to breathe looked up at the monster in the center of the room. The Barca Monster's head hung, the light gone from its eyes. The crystal orb fetus attached to its chest gave off smoke, and there were no signs of any life.

"At the same time as the curse was dispelled...?" Lulune whispered in a daze.

"...I don't know, but...the power of the curse has vanished..." Asfi responded in a quiet voice.

The people who had fallen to the floor coughing up blood started to rise—horribly battered, but the unhealable curse had disappeared from the air.

"Meaning...Amid beat the monster...?"

"...Idiot. That's not what...this is..."

Tiona's and Tione's voices rang hollow as the last act played out on the battlefield. It was unknown whether Amid's devotion had saved that one soul—whether Dea Saint's prayers had freed a single man from his thousand-year curse. Or whether he despised the girl for doing it. Regardless, the *D* in the monster's red eye had vanished.

"..."

Amid was kneeling on the floor, supported by the other two healers, her eyes shut as if grieving. Finally, she clasped her hands and offered up a silent prayer.

An unbefitting silence filled the room after the conclusion of the battle.

"...All right, prepare for the next move. Use all remaining items needed to heal Amid. We're re-forming with all those still able to fight. Hurry," urged Finn in a calm voice, directing them onward, not allowing them to immerse themselves in any lingering emotions.

They collectively raised their heads and started to move.

"We're splitting up! Don't let Thanatos escape! There's a high probability that a god by the name of Enyo will be present, too. Don't let any suspicious people get away!" Gareth boomed.

The location was the ninth floor of Knossos, an area far removed from where Finn and his group were fighting.

The great dwarf warrior looked out over the combined party of *Loki Familia* and *Dionysus Familia* members as he rattled off his commands.

"With their god present, this area shouldn't have as many monsters roaming around! Even if there are some, they won't be any bigger than the water spider ones! Those from *Dionysus Familia* should be able to handle them as long as you work in groups! Split up into as many teams as possible! We're going over every last bit with a fine-tooth comb!" he belted out.

With Lulune's directions, they had reached the major enemy base nearest the labyrinth master's room. Along with the main squad with the gods in tow, Gareth himself headed directly for the room, while the other teams searched the surrounding areas, to catch both Thanatos and whoever the mysterious Enyo ended up being. It was also Loki's divine will.

"That good?" Gareth asked with a glance.

"Perfecto!" The goddess with crimson hair flashed him an OK sign.

With a cheery attitude, Loki licked her lips as she strained her divine majesty. From there on, they could run into a god at any point.

"Squads! Make sure you have at least one dwarf with you! I'd expect them to have a secret path out for when their stronghold was about to fall! Don't miss any hidden passages!"

""Aye!"" The dwarves in both familias called back in response. Gareth nodded and finally turned to the elven mage for her orders.

"Lefiya, keep watch on the surroundings. Aiz might have lured out the red-haired creature, but the other masked one still hasn't shown up. If anything happens, report to me immediately."

"Y-yes, sir!"

He passed an oculus to Lefiya, who could use the same method as Riveria to search the surroundings for threats—by spreading *Rea Laevateinn*'s magic circle. It was an incredibly important role. Lefiya was nervous to take on the same responsibilities as one of the core members of the familia but accepted the oculus with determination and a sense of duty. She was ready to live up to that trust.

Gareth grinned as the members of both familias formed into parties.

"All right, let's go!"

The adventurers dashed off in all directions. The operation was at last reaching the final stages. They scattered into the surrounding areas to complete the task of taking down Knossos.

"____"

Amid all that, Dionysus paused at the entrance to a passage instead of moving with the main squad that contained Gareth and Loki.

It was a corridor shrouded in darkness, hidden in the shadows where the magical light of the wall-mounted lamps could not reach—a straight path becoming one with the void, unnoticed by the adventurers. There was no light ahead, and the darkness stretched out into the depths of the passageway even when Dionysus raised his handheld magic-stone lantern.

Somewhere in the depths of that darkness, something was quivering.

"…"

As if enticing Dionysus in…or ridiculing him.

His head ached. Dionysus swore he could smell the sweet scent of wine when he'd take it to his lips.

His heart thumped loudly—once. There was no longer anyone around him.

Looking to the side, he saw Loki and the others disappearing down the passage leading to the labyrinth master's room. When his gaze shifted back, he let his eyes fixate on the darkness before him. He realized his eyes flared in anger.

Holding one hand to his chest, he gripped the shortsword hidden away in his cloak. Taking the hilt designed in the shape of a grapevine, he drew the blade as if rousing himself to battle and took a step into the dark corridor.

"…Let's go, Filvis."

"Yes, Lord Dionysus."

He didn't bother looking back as his follower's response called out from behind him, as Dionysus quietly, seriously, resolutely started to proceed down the passage.

"…Why'd you go and die on me, Barca?"

Thanatos looked up. He was sitting on the pedestal, legs crossed, as he leaned back and supported himself with his hands.

One of his followers had stopped responding. It might have been one of the far-off, nameless soldiers whom he had promised a future beyond death. But he suspected that the soul that had left his side had been that of the man possessed by obsession. Aside from his fixation, Barca had been selfless and without desire—so pitiful, so ridiculous, so precious. Even among Thanatos's followers, he was a child who had particularly sparked his interest.

When Thanatos had taken the title of wicked god, taken part in the activities of the Evils, taken an unexpected pit stop at Knossos, Barca had already been there, already a prisoner of Daedalus in every sense of the term. He had been as pure and as cruel as a child, his soul more twisted than anyone's spirit, more than any soul Thanatos had ever seen before.

That was why the God of Death had loved Barca. To some extent, it could be said that he had been simply enjoying himself, but Thanatos had loved Barca in his own philosophical way.

His thoughts drifted to the heavens above, beyond the labyrinth where he was sealed away, with a minimal amount of sentimentality.

"...I thought everyone other than *Loki Familia* was just along for the ride, but...Dionysus's and Hermes's guys really got me."

There was no one left in the labyrinth master's room save Thanatos. They had all gone out to engage *Loki Familia* in battle. Even knowing they were no match, they were trying to buy time for their patron god to escape.

With his followers, he had made a contract that would be fulfilled with the destruction of Orario. So even if they were defeated here—as long as Thanatos could escape, as long as they gave him another opportunity to succeed—their dreams could be realized. That must have been what they believed.

"A decade or two is nothing to a god...but I really don't want to do all this again. Yeah, time flies, but it takes so much effort. It was trouble just getting this far...really..."

As the room fell silent again, Thanatos sighed heavily. Swinging his legs, he stood up from the pedestal. From that distance, he could make out the approaching footsteps of adventurers as he walked in the opposite direction, taking a different path to head into the darkness. He arrived at a location even deeper than the labyrinth master's room.

It was a wide room hosting a set of round pillars, as though the home of *Thanatos Familia* had nowhere to go aboveground.

The room was barely lit by small torches set into the pillars. On the back wall that was designated as an altar, there was an emblem with a heart made of iron and bronze and a black wing that resembled the God of Death's scythe.

In front of that altar, and at the bottom of the stairs, stood the person he was looking for, gazing up at the familia's emblem.

"Ein, my dear."

"..."

A masked person. A mysterious figure in the underground forces, called Ein by Levis and the others. As Thanatos stopped close to the silhouette and called out, the masked being wrapped in a purple-hooded robe gradually turned around.

"*Loki Familia got us. All my children have been defeated. There isn't anything left to do.*"

"..."

"Unleash the demi-spirits." That was all he said to the creature called a follower of the corrupted spirit.

There was no longer any way of stopping *Loki Familia*. They were already in check. The only possible way of turning things around was by using the *multiple* demi-spirits hidden away in Knossos.

Originally, the demi-spirits were intended to be the key to destroying Orario by summoning them aboveground. But given the gravity of the current situation, there was no use whining about that.

"*I refuse.*" Giving an unexpected response to Thanatos's request, the masked silhouette bluntly rejected him.

"You refuse...?"

"*The spirits have their own roles. They cannot be moved from their positions.*"

"Are you serious? Look at the situation. This isn't the time to be whistling past the graveyard."

"*It would go against Enyo's divine will.*"

Thanatos exhaled sharply as the voice somewhere between a man's and a woman's responded matter-of-factly.

He did not display irritation—but exasperation. "Even if you are

Enyo's puppet, there has to be a limit, right? What kind of farce would it be for the secret weapon to stay a secret to the end and never see the light of day?"

"..."

"Are you trying to say Enyo is a naked king on his throne?" he asked, a disparaging smile on his lips.

"*You are the fool,*" the masked being announced, cutting him off with the same cold, disinterested tone as before.

"_____"

"*No, you are a fool, too.*"

Backed by darkness, the figure's hooded robe quivered ominously as the silhouette continued. Thanatos froze in place.

"*A message from Enyo—'This is the end. Thank you for your cooperation.'*"

"...What...?"

"*I will complete the plan for the destruction of Orario. I shall open the path leading to the underworld. And in order to achieve that—*"

"*Become my sacrificial lamb, God of Death.*"

The chilling message rang through the dark room.

Thanatos could not move. He could not form a sentence. There was no shock, or agitation, or confusion. He did not even have time to feel humiliated from being looked down upon by a mortal. Because he was a god, he understood in an instant the true meaning of the masked figure's words—the divine will of the mastermind hidden within the message.

"*...Everything is as Enyo wills,*" the silhouette finished before slipping into the darkness.

Stillness closed in around Thanatos, an earsplitting silence gripping the god who was left behind.

Tick. He swore he heard the needle of a distant clock move.

"Gah...hah..."

Thanatos doubled over, letting out a sharp breath. And before he knew it, he couldn't control his emotions anymore as they exploded out of him.

"—Ha-ha-ha-ha-ha-ha-ha-ha-ha-ha-ha-ha! *Ha-ha-ha-ha-ha-ha-ha-ha-ha-ha-ha-ha-ha-ha-ha-ha-ha-ha-ha-ha-ha-ha-ha-ha!*"

His laughter broke the silence.

It kept going and going, as ceaseless as a broken music box, and his wild laughter echoed in the room as the shock rocked his body.

"Quit playing around! That's, like, when a god flaunting their omnipotence gets *slapped in the face with shame!*—Using me? Gimme a break!"

He cackled and guffawed—spilling out rage and self-derision as the one who understood what was happening in the labyrinth sooner than anyone else. A booming laugh containing his hatred, resignation, every last intense feeling.

"Come on. Don't give me that. Framing a nice guy like me?—Enyo, you piece of shit."

And at the end of it all, the loser crudely wiped the smile from his face, replacing it with a howling rage.

"—You're Thanatos, I take it?" called out a voice from behind him as he contained his laughter.

When he turned around, he was faced with a goddess with vermilion hair accompanied by a powerful dwarven warrior and some of her other followers. The patron gods of opposing factions stood before each other as though they had been intended to meet, as though they had been drawn together by a third party's design.

"We finally tracked you down, Thanatos."

"...Yes, I've been cornered, Loki."

Thanatos sneered as he murmured, "I can't go on like this" in a voice that Loki couldn't quite catch.

"Pick up the pace! Re-form the squad! There are still areas that need a key! We're setting up to attack again!" Finn fired off his orders.

He gathered the members of *Loki Familia* who had taken the least damage in the fight with the Barca Monster in order to move to their next target.

"If you've run out of items and other supplies, gather up and go back to replenish them. *Hermes Familia* set up a resupply route using the line of retreat that Aki secured with the others!"

The encirclement of the ninth floor was complete. Bete, Anakity, and Raul had pounced into action, securing the three different entrances to the Dungeon. According to the reports from the oculi, almost all the enemy forces had been wiped out already. The critical stairways had been secured with the help of *Dionysus Familia*.

Now that the Evils' resistance had been almost entirely pacified, Finn secretly raised a single crystal to his mouth. "How are things down there?"

"There were no problems on the eighteenth floor, Braver. As you said, I found the area where monsters were held. It's been cleared out according to plans. We've made it up to the thirteenth floor while destroying anyone in our path."

Fels was on the other end. Even though Finn had told the familia about the pact with the monsters, contacting this sage out in the open would just provoke those who still had hard feelings, which was why Finn quietly confirmed the situation and shared what was happening above.

"I had our group split up into two earlier, but the surroundings are entirely under control. There are no signs of Remnants or ambushes here. It's safe to assume we've severed any escape to the lower floors. What should we do? Continue on and try to confirm the demi-spirit's location ourselves?"

"Yes, please…Sorry, I'm going to break off now. If anything happens, contact me."

Upon noticing someone approaching, Finn ended the transmission with Fels.

"Captain Finn…I'm sorry for causing trouble."

"Amid, are you okay?"

"Yes, I can move now." Amid had walked over on her own two feet.

She had been bathed in a potent curse, but once she finally dispelled it, she had been able to restore herself.

But peering into her face, Finn knew what he had to order: "Amid, take the other healers and leave Knossos. Pull back out to the Dungeon."

"But—"

"We won't run into that strong of a curse again. Each squad has the anti-curse medicine to deal with anything we might encounter."

"…Understood."

She had won a grueling battle, but considering her body had been eaten away by a serious curse, he recommended that she retreat a bit early. Amid did not try to fight it, staying in her lane. Even though she had recovered, the healer recognized from an objective point of view that she would simply become a burden without her Mind and stamina at peak condition.

Amid was to go back with the group heading out to resupply. Until they were ready to depart, she spoke with Finn.

"Do you think there will be resistance from the enemy from here?"

"They can't turn things around through normal means for sure. To have a chance, they would have to unleash the demi-spirit to go on a rampage. But if they do that, it's our victory. We can simply pull back for now and prepare ourselves to finish it in the second attack."

All according to plan. If the enemy played their trump card, they would just follow their prepared plan. Finn had never expected to wipe out all their underground forces in the first attack. The goal of this first strike had always been to round up the Evils and get a firm grasp of Knossos's layout. The latter was basically complete now that they had Daedalus's Notebook, so if the stretch goal of dealing with the demi-spirit was pushed to the second operation, it wouldn't be a problem.

There was no need to get greedy now. Finn had no intention of stirring up trouble before the second attack.

From their conversation, Amid looked as though she understood. They had managed to basically achieve all they had set out to do with the first attack. There was no longer any way of changing that fact.

...That's how it should be...

But while he was speaking with Amid, he could not ignore the unease lurking in the back of his mind.

The enemy still hasn't made a move, even though it's come down to this. What's going on? Loki and Gareth are already closing in on Thanatos. At this rate, the Evils will be destroyed.

The enemy was responding too slowly. Even if they were to use the demi-spirit, it would be meaningless at this stage, now that *Loki Familia* had finished sealing off the floor. With escape routes secured, their alliance could either retreat or push onward at any point. Finn had planned for the possibility of the demi-spirit running wild and had put together various ways of countering, but all that effort had been wasted.

Maybe the enemy had not been able to deal with the speed of their advance—

Would it be fine for him to take this optimistic standpoint?

Then...internal turmoil? Maybe the underground forces and the creatures betrayed the Evils...But there's no reason to abandon them. To discard your own fighting force...

He combed through his mind, seeking out reasonable possibilities, but he could not find an obvious answer.

All that's left from their fighting force is Levis. Is there some way they could use her to turn things around? No, that just isn't realistic. And even if that wasn't what they were after, it would just be a tactical victory. The overall strategic trend is clearly in our favor.

None of it fit. They were all losing moves. All foolish plans.

Braver could not predict what the enemy was plotting. All the possibilities in his mind would be blunders, and yet he could not entirely discard them for one simple reason.

...My thumb...

Glancing down at his right hand, he maintained his silence. His right thumb was aching, an omen of something to come. Nothing intense, but it had been a continuous gnawing for a while now.

"...Amid, pull back the battle lines. Gather all those who have been wounded and bring them closer to the escape routes."

"Pull back? Are you sure?"

"Don't break the perimeter. Maintain it just enough so that the enemy can't escape. Gareth's squad is searching out the ringleaders, and we obviously can't pull them back, but...we should set up a line as a precaution for dealing with the demi-spirit, too. Tell everyone from *Hermes, Dionysus*, and *Dian Cecht Familias.*"

"Understood," Amid said as she bowed and left. Watching silently, Finn licked his thumb. He was unable to think of a plan that could resolve the mysterious unease lurking in his chest. He just could not picture the person moving the pieces on the other side of the board.

...Either way, pulling back our own forces at this stage is impossible.

They were in a position where they had no choice but to attack.

No choice but to push on to the end.

"...Tiona, Tione. Gather the best of all those who can still fight. We're going to attack with that group alone."

"Yes, sir! Leave it to us!"

"Collect the most hyped! Got it!"

Handing the Amazonian sisters their orders, Finn made his own preparations. He put together a squad with sufficient fighting strength to deal with any trap that might be lurking up ahead. Leading the familia members who had been gathered in an instant, Finn dashed off to the labyrinth master's room, where Gareth had headed with his squad.

Loki faced off with Thanatos.

With his long locks of deep-purple hair and androgynous features, he could pass for either a man or a woman. But more than anything, he gave off a uniquely degenerate vibe as the God of Death.

Standing there with no followers remaining, Thanatos smiled cynically at the situation.

"This is the first time we've met."

"Guess so. We didn't have any ties in the heavens, and I was always cooped up inside, managing the flow of souls."

"Well, this is a weird thing to say at our first meeting, but…this is the end, Thanatos."

"Yes, it's game over." He met Loki's sharpened gaze with a flippant smile.

While Gareth watched the gods' exchange in silence with the rest of the members of *Loki Familia*, Loki was getting suspicious. *He's too calm.*

Something was off about Thanatos. He was taking it too well. They had cornered him with ease, so she'd readied herself, assuming there was a hidden trick up his sleeve, but resignation seeped out of his every word. As if he had already abandoned the chessboard.

I can't put it into words, really, but…Yeah, it's like there's no reaction.

"Were you the one going by the name Enyo?" Loki questioned while carefully trying to conceal her doubts. But Thanatos just smiled and shrugged.

"Did you not ask dear Lefiya? I'm not Enyo at all."

"…"

"…Concealed from sight with a voice never heard. A god who may or may not even exist…An entity who may or may not even be a god. That isn't me…Speaking of, that enigmatic douche really pulled one over on me."

"…What?"

His smile took on a hint that he was mocking himself or maybe facing despair. Loki opened one of her eyes in surprise.

"Yeah, Enyo got me. Hook, line, and sinker. I wondered if they were playing some kind of game when they wouldn't even appear before me, but…it was all so I wouldn't notice. It's obvious, really. You can't get anywhere trying to probe someone's intentions if you never once meet them. Because we couldn't even begin *to outwit each other as gods.*"

——Couldn't outwit each other?

—Wait..."Got" him?

As Loki's thoughts ground to a halt, trying to process what he had said, Thanatos continued, "Enyo never thought of this place as a fortress. It was an altar. For a sacrifice."

Her body temperature dropped. A chill shot up her spine at the hint of a possibility that neither Finn nor she had been able to predict.

Her heart pounded. Hard.

An altar? A sacrifice? Where? Who? Here? Us?

In the back of her mind, a series of scraping noises rang out, chipping away at her feeling of discomfort—and giving way to a bright, flashing red warning of impending doom.

"Looks like *we were all* outwitted here, Loki."

Her eyes snapped open wide. The oculus in Gareth's hands suddenly let out a loud blare.

"*Mr. Gareth! The masked being...! It's controlling...monsters...too, and man—...! The squad i—...falling back...!*"

"Lefiya?! Lefiya! What's going on?! I can barely hear you!"

Her transmission cut between bloodcurdling screams, the violent clangor of battle, and the fiendish howls of monsters.

Loki did not take her eyes off Thanatos as she listened to it. Her thoughts were whizzing around her head at full speed. Imagining the board where they had commenced their fame, she scrutinized thousands, tens of thousands of moves in an instant. They had intended to put the enemy in check, but were they being manipulated by someone else? The board had been clearly pointing to their victory.

So who had *stabbed their sword down* from outside the board?

As if empathizing—or sympathizing—with Loki's internal revelation, a hint of compassion seeped into Thanatos's smile.

"Loki, were you by yourself when you came here? Didn't you have an important friend with you?"

"!"

His question made Loki finally realize that Dionysus was missing. After looking around in shock, she whipped out her oculus.

"Hey, Dionysus?! Where are you?!"

"Hey, Dionysus?! Where are you?!" rang the goddess's voice.

Dionysus brought the shining crystal to his mouth. "In one of the diverging passages…I apologize for moving by myself without consulting you. Please forgive me. I…am going to exact my revenge."

"What the hell are you talking about?!"

He tightened his grip on his shortsword as he spoke. In the jet-black passage, he relied on the faint flickering from the oculus for light, but he proceeded deeper without any fear.

"They're here. Up ahead. The mastermind behind it all…The accursed god who killed my children."

He was sure of it—of the fact that his enemy was almost before him.

His features were colored by rage. Knocking away the silence that coiled around him, he cut through the darkness with the light of his blade and kept moving.

Forward. He continued, as if sidling up to them, making sure not to lose sight of his target.

"…—?! Wait! Just wait, Dionysus!" she wailed, desperately trying to stop him in an uncharacteristically shaken voice from the crystal.

But Dionysus could not be stopped. He tailed the darkness beckoning him onward, as if driven by the flames of his wrath.

"Come back! It's seriously bad! I know something—something is about to happen! You can't be by yourself!"

The light from the crystal flashed brighter, as if strobing with the god's intuition. Loki's pleas rang hollowly in the open space. This place was filled with darkness—a somber, impenetrable black. And inside stood Dionysus's enemy.

"It's not a problem. I have Filvis," he said, fixing his gaze on the darkness ahead. "Right, Filvis?"

"Yes, Lord Dionysus."

Hearing the voice from behind him, he nodded.

"...Wait. Wait! Dionysus?!"

Checking his grip on his sword, Dionysus was about to launch out, hounding down the shadows—

"Just who were you talking to just now?!"

Her shout finally caused him to stop in his tracks.

"Ooooooooooooooooooooooooooooooooooh!"

"Gaaaaaaaaaaaaagh?!"

Voices cracked. Roars exchanged. A swarm of monsters with flailing tentacles and hideous jaws snapping routed the adventurers.

"Loose your arrows, fairy archers! Pierce, arrow of accuracy!——Arcs Ray!" Lefiya tried to fire back, but it was just a single drop in the bucket. Obviously.

After all, the masked being had descended on them with a giant flock of violas without any warning.

"Go."

"————*Aaaaaaaah!"*

The horde of monsters obeyed the fluttering purple robe, writhing in their serpentine way as they attacked the adventurers. Lefiya intentionally dispersed her magic power, trying to cover for the scattering adventurers by drawing the monsters' attention to her while using Concurrent Casting to finish them all off.

"!"

"Ugh?!"

The masked figure caught on and concentrated their attacks on her. With the enemy's attacks intensifying, Lefiya did not have the chance to continue talking to Gareth. The oculus picked up the sounds of the hectic clash between people and monsters.

A series of retreats caused the battlefield to keep shifting backward. She somehow managed to block the metal gloves, but the force behind them was inhuman, and she kept getting blown back.

"Lefiya?!"

At the sounds of battle, Anakity's squad ran to the scene, but it was too late. The masked figure was pressing in, pushing Lefiya all the way back to the entrance of the Dungeon that was secured by the squad of animal people.

"*This is the end.*"

Support from Anakity's squad wouldn't make it in time. The creature's tight fist was about to pound Lefiya with a fatal blow.

"*Dio Thyrsos!*"

A bolt of lightning flashed through the air, repelling the masked figure's attack just in the nick of time.

"Are you okay, Lefiya?!" asked a girl standing before her, barring the creature's way like a knight.

"*Miss Filvis!*" Lefiya rejoiced.

"_____"

Time stopped for Dionysus. When he halted and whipped around, the girl named Filvis Challia was not there at all.

All that was there was *darkness.*

The follower carrying a conversation with him had dispersed as though an illusion.

"*She isn't by your side at all! She's with Lefiya! She* can't *be there!*" Loki shrieked vehemently, parroting the news she had gathered from Lefiya's oculus.

Dionysus could not move. Dionysus could not understand.

She disappeared—just vanished.

No. Had she even been there to begi—?

"Yes, Lord Dionysus," rang out a voice in his ears, accompanied by an unpleasant static, before crumbling away like a sugary sweet illusion.

His expression cracked, warping his features in freakish confusion.

—Hah-hah-hah-hah.

An unpleasant gasping, a chaotic noise rustling against his ears.

He finally realized with a cold sweat that he was hyperventilating. That he was the source of the sound.

There was an entrancing darkness at Dionysus's side, creeping up on him. The labyrinth garbled as it bent, coiling its arm around Dionysus's body.

"...What...? What was...? What is...? *How?*"

Is this a hallucination? Or a daydream?

Impossible. I'm a god, one of the deusdea, omnipotent. There's no way sorcery should work on me. No way something of the mortal realm could deceive me. It isn't feasible. That would be impossible.

—It's not possible! Not possible! Not possible!

"Dionysus?! Dionysus!!"

He didn't know what was happening to his body.

Who is this place? What time am I? Where is the hour? Who are you?

The whole world flipped on its head. Context became unconsciousness. Order became chaos. And he became lost.

It was the beginning of a comedy, the start of a drama, an opera, a pantomime, a farce, a tragedy, a parody.

Dionysus the performer and Dionysus in the audience. Dionysus was the scriptwriter, the director, the stagehand. A bout of laughter accompanied thunderous applause. Ridiculing Dionysus from Dionysus's lips.

A toast! A toast! Here's a toast!

Tears dribbled onto his cheeks; drool streaked from the corner of his mouth; his cheeks blushed bright like a girl in love for the first time.

A headache that roared in the pitch of an animal. His personality ripped to shreds. His facade obliterated into smithereens.

Drink more. Drink more. Drink more.

Drunk on the darkness. Drunk on the darkness. Drunk on the darkness.

Ah, it's as if I've become...

Become a true fool.

"___"

And then, the darkness trembling, after keeping him waiting for so long.

Straight ahead. From the front. Right before his eyes.

The foe who Dionysus had been chasing gradually appeared before him, clutching a dagger.

Reflected in his eyes was a single divine figure.

"How ridiculous," the figure said, lips curling into a condescending crescent. The bewitching flash of the blade in their hand burned into Dionysus's eyes.

Impossible...It can't be...

The foe he'd pursued, the revenge that he'd sought, the true identity of Enyo...

"Dionysus!!" called out the goddess in the end.

Dionysus responded hollowly back.

"I'm sorry, Loki."

BOOOOOM!!

"What?"

Hestia saw *a pillar of light* reaching toward the sky, breaking through the labyrinth and shooting up into the heavens.

"The return of a god?!"

Aboveground on Daedalus Street, Ganesha was at his familia's camp, bellowing as he looked up at the pillar.

"Who? Who is it?!"

Shakti's shout rang out over the cries and confusion that raced through the familia in the blink of an eye.

"—Is it...?"

Hermes stood up, as if drawn in by the pillar. With just a couple of bodyguards by his side, the god watching over Knossos from the roof-top in the Labyrinth District looked on with eyes wide in surprise.

The giant pillar of light looked as though it had come from *inside* Knossos, not aboveground.

Its brilliancy was visible throughout the city, observable everywhere.

White and beautiful and grimly magnificent, the pillar of light stole the eyes of people and gods alike.

"————————————————————Gh?!"

A jerky rumble rocked the labyrinth. An enormous tremor, as if Knossos were at the epicenter of an earthquake. Everyone in the lab-yrinth staggered under this shock, regardless of location.

"I can't stand!" Asfi cried out as she struggled to stay on her feet.

"What haaappened?!" Falgar shouted in confusion, trying to cover Merrill and the others.

A collapse. An explosion. A flash of light. An overwhelming flow of information blotted out the adventurers' senses as a tsunami of destruction crashed through Knossos.

The stone slabs placed atop the adamantite structure crumbled, pitching down one after the other from the ceiling and the walls. The tremor shaking their vision up and down was incomparably more powerful than aboveground. An untold number of screams was drowned out by the intense swell of light.

"*Aaaaaaaaaaaaaaah?!*"

"*Oooooooooooooh————?!*"

The vividly colored monsters on the eighth floor and above that happened to be standing where the pillar of light *had passed through* were erased. All the violas and vargs, with no exceptions. Even the orichalcum gates were smashed to bits.

The torrent contained the most energy of anything that could be observed in the mortal realm. It was a heavenly phenomenon that tran-scended logic, a divine pillar that combusted everything that existed above it, destroying all in its wake.

The wave of light connecting heaven and earth diffused through the entirety of Knossos.

"Whoa, whoa, whooooa?!" Tiona shouted.

"Captain?!" Tione roared.

People collapsed over one another, and the prum leader thrust his spear into the stone floor and shuddered at the chaotic irregularity.

My thumb—!

An unrivaled ache throbbed in his finger.

From a temporal standpoint, it didn't last that long.

But for those caught in the epicenter, the roaring rush of light felt endless before the radiance rising to the heavens finally faded and reached its end.

"Is…it over…?"

The thundering quieted down, and the quakes subsided.

In a large passage, Lefiya had managed to endure the shock and lifted her head. The surrounding scene was ghastly. Other than the floor, all the stone slabs had been shaken loose, and the metallic luster of adamantite sparkled all around them. The magic-stone lamps on the walls had all shattered on the ground, giving off a blue phosphorescence at their feet. Lefiya looked around in awe at it all.

"Lefiya, prepare yourself! The enemy is still here!"

"—Gh?!"

And though the battle had been paused, the enemy stood before her, appearing unfazed.

Lefiya could feel Anakity's shout pelting against her back. The masked figure leading the violas stood there as if a shadow, facing them. Ignoring the monsters whose dull roars of fear or excitement hung in the air, the creature showed no sign of withdrawing. In fact, they were calmly observing the adventurers of *Loki* and *Dionysus Familias. As if everything was going exactly as planned.*

Behind her, Anakity drew her sword with a sharp scrape, and the others followed her lead, as Lefiya immediately readied herself, preparing to deal with the danger before her even though she still had not processed the situation.

"Ah…Aaaah…" Next to her, a single girl trembled.

"Miss Filvis…?"

She was staring down at both her hands, eyes wide. Lefiya could not understand what it meant at first. But noticing the state of the members of *Dionysus Familia* in the surroundings, she ceased all movement.

"No way..."

"Th-this is...You're kidding me...?"

"It can't be...?!"

The color drained from the faces of Dionysus's followers. Some were looking down at their hands, as Filvis was, some were holding themselves tight, and some were frozen, as if despairing over something that had been lost.

As if something important had been taken from inside them—

"*A god's disappeared.*"

When Lefiya froze, the masked figure let their purple robe billow.

"What?"

"*Loki or Thanatos...or Dionysus.*"

Those words carried a certain meaning.

Time stood still for Lefiya as she realized what had happened.

But there was no way to turn back the clock.

"Aaaah...aaaah...aaaaaagh...!" Filvis let a scream fall from her lips, hit with reality, crushed by despair.

And after the scratchy scream managed to force its way out of her parched throat, her body started to convulse.

Was it with rage or hatred—or sadness or anguish?

Lefiya went rigid. Next to her, the elf shrouded in white took a step forward, taking the form of a ghost—or Banshee, her taboo name.

It was as if she were possessed by something. As if she had lost her home and gotten beaten down.

"*Everything is according to Enyo's will. Rejoice, sisters—the farce is at its end.*"

In the next instant, the girl let out a piercing shriek from the back of her throat.

"—*AAAAAAAAAAAAAAAAAAAAAAAAAAAAAAAAAAAAAAA AAAAAAAAAAAAH?!*"

In her startled state, Lefiya was unable to react quickly enough to stop her. Her outstretched hand caught air as Filvis lunged at her sworn enemy.

"Miss Filvi…" She trailed off partway.

Slow. Too slow.

Filvis was so slow that it was almost laughable.

Her patron god had returned to the heavens. Her Status had been sealed.

The followers of a late god could not wield their enhanced abilities without first converting to a new deity. The Blessing engraved on her back had fallen silent in accordance with the contract.

The fairy consumed by fervid emotion had become nothing more than a normal person.

Seconds stretched out. Sounds grew distant. For some reason, Lefiya was confronted by all her memories with this girl, flashing through her head, with no logical connection between each scene.

Their first encounter when the girl had rejected her, the callous way she had tortured and defiled herself, smile that had bloomed when Lefiya had taken her hand—

Why?! Why?! Why am I remembering this now?!

Lefiya refused to acknowledge what this phenomenon meant, howling in her head as she kicked the ground with all her might, stretching her arm toward Filvis's back.

But before she could reach her, the masked figure's metal glove flashed, closing around the girl's slender neck.

The five metal fingers snaked around, interlocking in place.

The svelte legs of the elf lifted from the ground, yanked up by a single hand.

"Gragh—"

As time ticked forward in slow motion, that was the only thing Lefiya could still hear clearly.

She didn't even realize there was incomprehensible garble pouring from her own mouth.

Dangling the girl by the throat, the masked being looked almost bored as force entered that grip.

And just like the culprit who had slain Dionysus's other children, approaching from the front, gripping their necks, and snapping them—as if this enigmatic enemy had taken their lives that very same way—

"Stoooooo—!"

In that moment, for just an instant, Lefiya felt the gaze of her scarlet eyes through her swaying black locks.

Almost as if she was apologizing.

Crack.

Tragic. Simple.

A snap rang out.

Her head tilted forward unnaturally.

Her limbs dangled as though they belonged to a doll whose strings had been cut. The murderer's devilish hand squeezed tight, covering her slender neck from view.

The members of *Loki Familia* trembled.

The members of *Dionysus Familia* went rigid.

And total emptiness filled the mind of Lefiya Viridis.

Time stopped. Color drained from the world. Every last emotion bled out of her, and she lost control of herself.

And then the creature tossed Filvis's body aside, as if losing interest. She was flung through the air, her arms and legs trailing behind her like a rag doll.

The creature had fed her to a viola.

In one gulp—it swallowed her whole, like a red fruit.

Under a light shower of blood, something fell between Lefiya and the creature.

A single arm.

Filvis's slender arm in its white sleeve.

And then her open wound suddenly sprayed a fountain of blood, as if remembering it was no longer attached to her body.

A moment of silence.

The final tick before the frozen seconds burst forward at last.

In the next instant, Lefiya's heart shattered.

© Kiyotaka Haimura

"*AAAAAAAAAAAAAAAAAAAAAAAAAAAAAAAAAAA*
AAAAAAAAAAAAAAAAAAAAAAAAAAAAAAAAAAA
AAAAAAAAAAAAAAAAAAAAAAAAAAAAAAAAAAA
AAAAAAAAAAAAAAAAAAAAAAAAAAAAAAAAH?!"

An earsplitting wail, ripping apart her vocal cords. A lamentation, nothing like a requiem. A shriek, unleashing unformed magic power even though she hadn't chanted anything.

Anakity and the others were forced to cover their ears.

The masked figure did not stir in the slightest. Instead, the arm that hit the ground sent ripples across the surface of pooling blood.

And as if responding to her grief—or rather, *in sync with the god's return*, the altar was activated.

"*Laaaaaaa―――...*" echoed twistedly beautiful singing voices.

Despite their corrupted forms, the spirits exchanged a chorus that trembled as if they were receiving a divine edict. The six voices overlapped in harmony.

The demi-spirits that had been placed around Knossos were connected along the perimeter of the giant pillar of light—causing their bodies to swell disgustingly.

A hideous noise burbled as *green flesh poured out* of their colossal bodies as though wombs giving birth.

In the next moment, the green flesh started to erode its surroundings at a dreadful speed.

"H-hey! What's that?!"

"Is that...a monster?!"

The first to spot it were the adventurers from *Dionysus Familia* who had taken up positions at the stairs leading down to the tenth floor.

The grotesque mass of flesh seeped up out of the stairs as a tremor shook the labyrinth.

"Hah—Gaaaaaaaaaaaaaaaaaaaaaaaaaaaaaaaaaaaaaaaagh?!"

Those who drew their swords and those who turned to run faced the same end, as it was all futile.

From the floor, the walls, the ceiling, the rushing stream of flesh filled every nook and cranny, swallowing up adventurers. Gulping them down and turning them into nourishment—absorbing and hunting. It was overrunning everything. To the fleeing adventurers, it was the jaw of a man-eating monster that cackled in delight as it consumed more people.

"Gaaaaaaaaaaaaaaaaaaaaaaaaaaaaaaaaaaaaaaaaaaaaaaaaaaaaaaaa aaaaaaaaaaaaaaaaaaaaaaaaaaaaaaaaaaaaaaaaaaaaaaaaaaaaaaaaah?!"

The surviving soldiers from the Evils' Remnants were consumed without ever knowing what was happening.

The same scene unfolded all around the labyrinth.

Once one was swallowed by the wave of flesh, there was no hope of escape.

A male animal person and the elf girl he'd been attempting to help, who'd tripped over her feet, were ground up together. A human boy sacrificing his comrades to try to get away was gobbled up by the wall of green flesh closing in from the front. The green mass pervaded the passages at an abnormal rate, a torrential flood in an enclosed space, drowning out the death throes of adventurers and cries of monsters as it turned the enormous labyrinth into a fleshy casket in the blink of an eye.

Diverging paths, stairs, pits—there were no exceptions to where it filled.

"Retreeeat! Retreeeeeeeeeeeeeeat!"

All the adventurers sprinted away as fast as they could, accompanied by pandemonium. Casting aside their weapons and shields, abandoning their positions, they lost their minds as the green flesh closed in from the sides, thrusting themselves into whatever paths remained to escape.

"B-Beeeeeeete?!"

"Get outside!" bellowed the werewolf from the middle of the squad of animal people.

"Hurry! To the Dungeon!" shouted the holy woman who had abandoned her composure.

"Fels?!"

"Retreat! To the gate! Quickly!"

"—Gh!"

"Wh—?! Wait! Rei!"

Even the heretical monsters beat a retreat at full speed.

"Th-this is…the same stuff that we saw at the pantry on the twenty-fourth floor…?!"

"Lulune! Ruuuuun!"

Hermes Familia had seen something similar at the pantry on the twenty-fourth floor. It was the plant that the creature Olivas Act had spoken about.

The main difference was that this was more violent, overwhelming, and merciless than that plant. It was squeezing the life out of every single living thing in its range.

It started re-forming Knossos from the tenth floor, completely ravishing Daedalus's thousand-year obsession.

Barca Perdix had been fortunate. Even though he had not been able to see his delusion through to its completion, at the very least, he had managed to die without seeing it end in this manner.

"Run! All of you, run!"

The green mass was closing in on Aiz and the rest on the twelfth floor. Riveria had shouted as the surging wave of green erupted from the various passages connecting to the room. She shoved the backs of the screaming familia members away from it. As they rushed into the one remaining open passage, Aiz flashed a glance at the red-haired woman with a trembling gaze.

"You knew it would end up like this from the start…didn't you?!"

Levis had only stared at them the entire time, never once attempting to cross blades with them in the end.

She scoffed disinterestedly. The onrushing wave of flesh approached her from all sides, but the moment it got within a certain distance of her, its movement slowed. It avoided her, forming a gap of space, as if to avoid hurting its own kind.

"It would be inconvenient for these clones to absorb you for food… They're disposable, after all," Levis coolly announced as Aiz gazed in wonder. "I was told it didn't matter if you were dead or alive, but it wouldn't be satisfactory to bring you back all withered up. Hurry up and scram, Aria."

"…?!"

"I'll finish this next time."

With that, Levis melted into the green flesh.

"Aiz, what are you doing?!"

"…Gh!"

Riveria's yell came at her from behind.

Unleashing her wind to full, Aiz darted away from the oncoming wall of flesh.

The adventurers scrambled—dashing away from a nightmare from which they would never again wake.

They leaped out of the gates connecting to the ninth floor of the Dungeon that they had secured. With Finn's instructions—or rather, with his intuition—they had pulled back their battle lines, allowing many adventurers to escape by the skin of their teeth.

However, there was one exception: *Dionysus Familia*. With their Falna sealed, they had lost their superhuman abilities, rendering them unable to avoid the green flesh's unrestrained approach. In a deadly predicament that even upper-class adventurers struggled to get through, it was logical that those who had become normal people would not make it out.

"Aaaaaaaaaah! Aaaaaaaaaaaaaaaaaaaah?! Aaaaaaaaaaaaaaaagh?!"

"No! Lefiya?!"

In the main passage, Anakity desperately stopped Lefiya, weeping hard, as she stretched out her hand toward the tragic arm on the floor.

Wrapping her arm around the girl losing herself in an unending torrent of tears, Anakity darted her eyes around when she saw the green flesh finally approaching them.

The first victims were, of course, *Dionysus Familia*. Their screams of despair rang out as they were taken in by the maelstrom of flesh.

"Help! *Loki Familiaaaaaaaaa*?!"

The exit was right there. It wasn't far to get into the Dungeon.

The masked being wasn't attacking, only observing them quietly, letting them go, as if savoring this moment.

And yet, and yet, and yet, saving everyone was impossible.

If they tried to carry the people from *Dionysus Familia*, who had effectively become dead weight, Anakity and all the familia members behind her would—

"—*Gh!*" Faced with that decision, Anakity abandoned them.

As she bit her lip, heartbroken, she deafened her ears to the voices begging to be saved, turning her back on their outstretched hands. Lifting Lefiya, she sprinted.

It wasn't just her, either.

In many places, people were forced to abandon the comrades next to them, shedding untold tears, apologizing over and over.

"Wait! Waiiiiiii—?!"

"Noooooooooooooooooooooooooooooooo?!"

It was a chain reaction of cries.

"It can't b—...Everyone...Filvis...Lord Dionysuuuuuus?!"

Their second-in-command, Aura, was devoured by the green flesh.

The fates of all those who had borne the name Dionysus were no different.

And that included even the dismembered arm that had been left behind.

"The return of a god was the switch to activate the altar...It didn't matter who blasted off."

In a room where round columns soared high, Thanatos had mumbled aloud as Loki and the others were knocked around by the tremors of Knossos, trying to process the current situation.

"A switch?! A god's return?! What are you talking about?!" Loki yelled.

"The demi-spirits are already at work. You can try to escape, but that won't do anything, Loki. Even if you have no clue what's happening…you can at least realize that it'd be futile, right?" Thanatos smiled dully.

Unable to say anything in response, she gritted her teeth.

"Loki!!" thundered out the prum.

"Finn?!" Loki's eyes were wide as she swung around.

The party of *Loki Familia*'s elites had set out for the labyrinth master's room to save their patron god and had made it all the way to this place.

"A gross meat thing is closing in!!"

"If we don't hurry, there won't be any way out!!"

Tiona and Tione were more uneasy than they had ever been before.

The low rumbles of the labyrinth never ceased.

The others, including Gareth, were totally lost, but they could immediately piece together that something big was happening. As if responding to their confusion, it burst into the room with force.

"C-Captain?! Incoming!!" someone shouted as the green flesh pushed through the passage.

"Close the door!!" Finn roared.

That was enough for the others to immediately understand everything.

Loki was stupefied by the shock. The familia member with the Daedalus Orb held it out, lowering the orichalcum gate. The door slammed shut, halting the invasion of the flesh by a hairbreadth. Of the five passages leading into the room, four doors crashed down with a *BOOM! BOOM! BOOM! BOOM!*

"What a shame, Braver. One of the entrances to this room doesn't have a door."

"——Gh!"

The green flesh rushed into the room from the remaining entrance as Thanatos mercilessly handed down their death sentence.

The prum's blue eyes went unfocused; the familia members paled; the first-tier adventurers realized their end was upon them. The flesh expanded out as if a malignant tumor, filling the pillar room within seconds and pressing into *Loki Familia*.

"I-is it swallowing up weapons, too?!"

"Our magic blades don't do anything!"

The desperate resistance of familia members was meaningless. Even as lightning and explosions overlapped, the green flesh did not slow its advance in the slightest. They retreated bit by bit until they were finally forced back onto the altar where Thanatos stood.

As they heaved ragged breaths, sweat pouring from their brows, despair was evident on everyone's faces. The heart made of iron and bronze and the emblem with the black wing, the symbol of the God of Death, hung over them, as if proclaiming their impending doom.

"—If Loki gets bounced out of the mortal world here, Orario will be destroyed without too much trouble."

That was when Thanatos shut his eyes and started his monologue.

"…?"

"If I leave the destruction of the city to Enyo, the mortal realm will be restored to its former chaos. The souls returning to the heavens will heighten, and my desires will come true, too," he spoke eloquently.

His calm voice sounded out of place in their current situation. It was almost like he was delivering an oracle. As he turned away from the altar, everyone bore their eyes into his back.

Was it a verse offered in tribute to the adventurers before they met a tragic fate? A proclamation of victory?

It did not sound like either to Loki. It was as if—

"—This shit isn't funny."

Sure enough, when Thanatos opened his eyes, there was a smoldering rage burning in them.

"Even I've got some pride, Enyo. I hate getting manipulated and cast aside."

"Thanatos…?"

"All that's left is…retaliation." At that, the God of Death broke into a smile. "A little payback for doing this to the dream of my dear Barca."

Loki caught her breath. At the end of it all, she had gotten a glimpse of Thanatos's love for his followers.

In the next moment, Thanatos drew a shortsword. As Finn and the others looked on in horror, he grinned and plunged it into his own chest.

"Wha—?!"

With a cough, blood started to ooze out of his mouth. The blade was thrust deep into his chest. While they speechlessly watched, the fatally wounded body of a god activated his Arcanum that was forbidden to him in the mortal realm, as if rejecting death.

"—Go, Loki. A present from me."

Her eyes opened wide. In the end, as he was surrounded by light particles and his figure blurred by the light that he emanated, Thanatos raised a single hand, pointing to the sky.

BOOM!

A second return pillar pierced the ceiling and rushed out of Knossos.

The force created a cascade moving in reverse up toward the heavens. As if shriveling back from a god's divine authority, the green flesh's encroachment slowed while the white light illuminated the shocked faces of the adventurers.

And then, because the giant pillar of light had burst through the labyrinth to the sky, *it had opened a route to get back aboveground.*

"—Escape through that hole! Nooooooooooooow!" Loki shouted as she confirmed the big hole in the ceiling from the fading pillar.

The first-tier adventurers started moving, perhaps even before she had said anything. It was a reflex to escape the threat of total annihilation. Without thinking, Tiona, Tione, and Gareth instinctively grabbed the familia members with the lowest Statuses. Accelerating fast enough to shatter the stones as they kicked off, they leaped up into the hole filled with snowy particles of light.

"Loki!!"

"—!"

As the other adventurers dropped their gear and followed the trio, Finn yanked Loki and charged above. In the next instant, the invasion of the green flesh started anew, as if intent on not letting them escape.

"Jump! Jump! Juuuuump!"

The adventurers gave no thought to appearances, screaming as they kept leaping, like a bolt of lightning zigzagging between floors, going up through the openings, pushing farther and farther upward. They were all desperately aiming for the light above their heads, for the starry twilight, for an escape from the lair of demons.

"Gah…!"

The air was electric, and the atmospheric pressure tugged at his skin.

Finn's shoulder creaked as it held Loki, on the verge of dislocating. But he did not have any thought to spare to protest or cry out in pain. There was no point in groaning.

As he looked down, he could see the repulsive green flesh hounding them, an eruption bursting before his eyes.

It would end if they got caught in it. It would all have been for naught.

"Finn!"

"Hurry!!"

Tiona and Gareth were at the head of the escape, calling back to Finn, who was bringing up the rear. While the other familia members desperately tried to put distance between themselves and the onrushing flesh, the prum supporting Loki managed to find another reserve somewhere in his small frame and accelerated again as he leaped.

And they finally closed in on the surface, right as he was crossing over to the second floor of Knossos.

"Oooooooooooooooooooooh—!"

The howl of a monster thundered from his side.

"_____"

In the second-floor passage, a single viola had managed to escape the pillar of light. Right as Finn and Loki were passing through, almost as if it was a trap that had been set for them, the monster opened its mouth to take a bite out of them.

"_____"

As Loki tensed, Finn arrived at a decision faster than light, executing his next actions immediately. He heaved his patron goddess into the air above his head with his right hand, *leaving her* to Tione above him in one second. And in the next, he used the Fortia Spear in his left hand to disembowel the approaching viola.

As time stood still for everyone else, those two seconds were fateful for Finn. The green flesh closing in from behind roared as the pitiful prum sank into its inescapable range.

"_____"

To deal with the attack, his upward momentum had slowed slightly. With his body weightless in the air for a split second, there was no possible movement that he could make to overcome it.

Gareth's eyes widened as their gazes met.

Tiona looked aghast as she exchanged glances with him.

Loki's gaze pierced through his as she tried to scream something.

Tione locked eyes with him as a chill ran up her spine.

And in the end, the ache in his thumb stopped entirely, as if finally giving up on everything.

"Captaaaaaaaaaaaaaaaaaaaaaaaaaaaaaaaaaaaaaaaaaaaaaaaaaaain!!" shrieked Tione.

Paying her grief no mind, the green flesh closed in.

The blue eyes of the prum filled with regret as he looked up, and all too quickly, it started to swallow him.

"——I won't let you."

In the last moment, a pair of golden wings swooped in and snatched his body from the clutches of the green flesh.

"Huh?" Tione whispered as Finn's eyes opened wide.

Loki and the other adventurers were all stunned.

A single Xenos had appeared.

The winged monster had accelerated from the room at the bottom through the tiny gap between the erupting flesh and the wall, saving Finn from a certain death.

Casting off Fels's restraint, Rei the siren had used her echolocation to search for survivors and, upon reaching the room with the altar, rushed to the adventurers. Whizzing through the air to avoid the green flesh's menace, her talons gripped firmly into Finn's arm.

"We're getting out of this!"

It was an explosive speed, something that only a being with wings could achieve. Tione and the others gazed in wonder as the siren burst past them in an instant with Finn in tow—and then put in every last bit of energy and leaped.

To the end of the tunnel, hurtling out aboveground.

"—Gh!!"

They passed through the gaping hole and up into the night sky. The half-human, half-bird silhouette flapping her golden wings floated together with the silhouette of a prum, the full moon shining behind them.

"_____!!"

The green flesh flooded out of the hole with a thunderous clamor as though a monster's roar. The crater opened up by Thanatos's return to the heavens was completely closed off, filled with its unsightly meat. As Tione and the others landed in the Labyrinth District, they frantically scurried away from the geyser of green mass burbling out of the hole.

"…It…stopped…"

The repulsive mass spread out to a radius of about ten meders before coming to a halt. As if perfectly sealing a lid over the altar.

"…"

With his arm gripped by the siren's talons, Finn squinted as he looked down from the sky. It was his first time observing the city from a bird's-eye view, but the scene before him was a bitter one.

Finally, he turned his gaze above his head and opened his mouth.

"…My thanks."

"…It was nothing."

The human and monster exchanged words of gratitude. However, even that could do nothing more than resound hollowly across the night sky.

On that day, the first attack of the Knossos assault operation succeeded—and *failed*.

They had achieved their goal of crushing the Evils. And Thanatos, the patron god of the Evils, had been sent back, too. But the cost had been the destruction of *Dionysus Familia*.

The alliance of familias had retreated—no, they had been routed. Far too many lives had been lost to call it a fair trade.

The den of demons cleared by adventurers had turned into the stronghold of a new devil.

Whodunit

Гэта казка іншага сям'і.

дэтэктыўны раман

Approximately eighty people and one god.

That was the number of casualties in this operation.

Loki Familia and *Hermes Familia* both suffered losses, but they had managed to keep their death toll down to zero. It could be said that they had minimized losses as best as possible when faced with an unforeseen Irregular—but that had been achieved only at the cost of abandoning *Dionysus Familia.* There was no helping the drop in morale. Though it was the first time that their familias had teamed up, losing an entire familia was far too heavy of a burden.

Though they took care not show it to the lower-tier members, the second-string members charged with command during the operation, including Anakity, were steeped in gloom.

And the one who had been hit particularly hard was Lefiya.

Seeing her fellow elf and friend perish before her eyes had ripped out the young girl's heart. With a broken spirit, she did not react at all to the beckoning of Aiz or anyone, simply sitting in her room like a lifeless doll.

Out of consideration for her roommate, Elfie, who had been reduced to tears trying to cheer her up countless times, Lefiya had been moved to a different room.

All the preparations for taking on Knossos had been lined up. And right when they succeeded, it had all been undone in a single devilish act.

There was no denying it. Not for the adventurers and not for the gods.

They had underestimated Enyo, who had not once stepped out onto the main stage.

Their enemy was exceedingly crafty: a devil incarnate.

*　　*　　*

"..."

The morning after the operation, Loki was on Daedalus Street. By herself, without any guard atop a building's roof in the central area of the Labyrinth District—looking out at Knossos.

The green flesh from before had overflowed aboveground through the openings made from Thanatos's and Dionysus's returns. It was being covered up with a giant tent that had been erected under the pretense of building a forest park in the reconstructed zone—to prevent normal residents from finding out about any disturbances.

Its corrosion of Knossos was total. With a few others, Bete had worked quickly to close the orichalcum doors connecting to the Dungeon, stopping the hemorrhaging. It had overflowed in only two places: the two holes where the gods had returned to heaven in the center of the Labyrinth District.

The green mass had fallen entirely silent now. Or perhaps it was better to say that its growth had stopped.

"When Leene died with the others, I guess I went out on a lookout then, too..." she let fall from her lips, the whisper disappearing in the morning breeze.

Ganesha Familia was stationed around the edges of the tent, the subject of Loki's attention, to investigate and observe it. She could see their leader, Shakti, shooting off constant orders to the other familia members without any sleep or rest, and even their patron god, Ganesha. If anything were to happen to Loki, they would surely come running. They were on their toes, and anything could set them off.

"......" Gazing over the Labyrinth District from the roof, Loki finally took her hand off the rail.

She headed down the stairs, slipping around to the back alleys to get away from the bustle of the adventurers.

"Yo, Loki. What a coincidence. What a way to start off the morning."

"..." She ran into Hermes.

Loki did not respond to the god who appeared as if he had been waiting for the chance to talk. She just silently looked back at him.

"Care for some small talk?"

"Fine, I'll bite. Just get to the point." She shrugged.

After Hermes finished distancing his following guards, the smile on his suave face melted away.

"I'd like to hear your opinion on the identity of Enyo." He met her gaze with a serious look in his orange eyes.

"Same as what you're thinking. Not like there was that much to go off."

"True. We know way too little. No leads on Enyo. No way to guess at a motive. It's all a blank."

The only thing they did know was Enyo's screwy name: the city destroyer.

Their enemy's existence was a vague shadow, some indefinite being. They weren't even sure whether Enyo actually existed. Because of that, they had not really tried to track down Enyo.

More accurately, they couldn't.

But an actual enemy had now bared its fangs at them with malice, posing a real threat. As if loudly asserting its existence. As if cackling at them.

"All right, let's say who we thought Enyo was on three?" Hermes suggested with a smile in an about-face.

But his eyes weren't smiling. Loki nodded silently.

Without taking her eyes off Hermes's lips as he counted down—"Three, two, one"—she answered.

""Dionysus.""

The same name hung in the air.

Their expressions didn't falter at the fact that their guesses had been the same.

"Why him?" Loki asked.

"His timing was too perfect. His motive for getting wrapped up and involved with you…it all felt like an after-the-fact explanation. At the least, that's how it looked to me," Hermes answered without any hesitation. "Did you know? After the incident on the twenty-fourth floor, the very first person I contacted was Dionysus."

"...You saying you suspected him from the start?"

"I wasn't convinced by any means. But I poked around a bit."

He was speaking with his usual nonchalance, but Loki had felt it, too.

Dionysus had been too active.

Before the Twenty-Seventh-Floor Nightmare, his faction had been one scrapping for the top spot in the city, but after, it was solid mid-tier, with its fairly numerous members as its only defining feature. He had apparently been very secretive with his familia and made a point of hiding their true strength, but he was still way out of his league to take on the remnants of the Evils and the creatures' underground forces. That could be proven by the fact that he had the assistance of only the Level-3 Filvis Challia up until the assault operation itself.

"Dionysus and I come from the same homeland...sworn friends of Olympus. I probably know him better than you do."

"You mean his sudden fits—getting into huge scuffles with folks?"

"Oh, you knew?"

There were other suspicious points, too: his extreme opposition to Ouranos that hindered their cooperation. They wouldn't have been able to make a deal with Ouranos's side while he was hiding the bombshell about the Xenos, but even then, Dionysus was stubbornly against them.

"Back in the old days, Dionysus had a volatile personality. If he had actually settled down once he came here, then he was in the middle of the uproars *too often*."

The god concluded: that was why he had proposed an alliance—to observe Dionysus.

"Mind if I ask a question now? If you suspected him, why bring Dionysus along during the assault on Knossos?"

"...For one, he never let enough slip to give me a reason not to take him. Also, once he was in the enemy's base, I figured he would try to pull something—even if he thought he was being careful and patient...and we could at least control the situation if he was with us."

And she had told Gareth on the down low, in case of an emergency.

However, Dionysus had managed to pull away from Loki—of all things that he could have done.

"Plus…I couldn't totally doubt him."

"…"

"I've got a good nose for fishy business, too, but…I couldn't smell it from him."

That was Loki's honest opinion. There was definitely something suspicious about his behavior. However, his determination and the divine will behind it were real—or at least that was how it had felt to Loki.

The decisive point had been the other day. She had not been able to find it in herself to doubt the vow that he'd sworn in front of his followers' graves.

"Dionysus said the real deal…At least, it felt that way to me. If that really was just manipulation, then all I can say is he got me."

"If it was enough to get you to say that…then I guess our suspicions about Dionysus were just bias and unfounded doubts?"

"There's enough blame to go around. He acted pompous and shady, too."

"True," Hermes responded with an easy smile and looked up at the sky.

"Sorry for suspecting you…Dionysus."

He cast his gaze up to the heavens to where the god had just ascended.

"Feeling guilty?"

"Ha-ha. As if."

Hermes looked toward the ground and placed his finger on the brim of his hat, pulling it down to cover his eyes. Or so Loki thought, but then he leaned in close to Loki, and she could see his piercing gaze peeking out from just below the edge.

"You see, Loki…I'm mortified."

"…"

"We were totally *duped*. That's what this was. Dionysus was the scapegoat, drawing our attention and keeping us on each other's cases while the mastermind bought time to move around in secret. Yeah. I don't know which god it was yet, but I'm so mortified that I can barely stand it."

Hermes certainly didn't feel anything as cute as guilt. The eyes peering into Loki's face brimmed with rage. Coming to terms with the reality that he had been manipulated, he was utterly chagrined.

"What about you, Loki? I'm just a phony, but…they even led you, the heavens' ultimate trickster, around by the nose. Is there anything more shameful than that?"

Hermes backed away, lifting his hands palms up, as if it was all a joke.

She would be lying if she denied it. But even she was at a loss for how to describe the feeling that waxed and waned in her heart as though a dry wind blowing through its gaps.

"…Well, either way. Now I know you're thinking along the same lines as I am. I'm going to try looking into things connected to Dionysus."

"Another one of your investigations?"

"Yeah. Starting now, I'm looking for the ringleader."

With that, Hermes walked off. As he passed, he slipped a chess piece into Loki's hand—the black king.

"…"

After he disappeared, Loki leaned back against the wall of the alley, securing the black king, the piece that represented Enyo, before turning up her head. A blue sky spread above the city. It was clear, without a single cloud, as if nothing had happened.

"Why the hell'd you have to go and ascend for…?" Loki murmured suddenly as she looked at the sky, carved into shape by the buildings lining the alley—speaking to the god who had disappeared into it alongside so many of his followers.

"Were you really being manipulated, Dionysus…?"

There were no longer any fragments of the pillar in the blue sky, and even though she asked, no answer would be coming.

Was Dionysus looking down on Loki from the heavens? Or did

all the gods up there peeping on the mortal realm see through everything?

Maybe they were pointing and having a good laugh at Loki of all people for being pathetic. Normally, she would get pissed at the thought of that, but for some reason, she just did not feel like that now.

"…"

That sentimentality was not like her. Shaking it off, she emulated Hermes: not looking back at things gone past but continuing to move forward. For the time being, she gave it a thought.

Was Dionysus played for a fool? In order to draw our attention, as Hermes was saying…? If so, why was Dionysus dancing to Enyo's tune? Why did…? No, how did they manage that?

That was what was bothering Loki. If it was like that, then a theory where Dionysus was connected to Enyo made more sense.

Based on Hermes and the shrimp, Dionysus definitely had some extreme tendencies. Like how I used to be.

Gnawed by the poison of boredom, he had contracted the rare illness that afflicted gods. Loki had been the same, getting into knock-down, drag-out fights with gods.

"That time when he was about to get into it over that title…the Twelve Gods, I think? Was anyone other than those twelve involved in it—?"

Thinking that far, Loki suddenly changed her perspective.

What if…what if…Dionysus was being manipulated back then? What if he was being controlled to have extreme outbursts, set up to be scapegoated…to be a cover for Enyo to move around in secret?

Loki could not even laugh as she weaved together that speculation. She sunk into thought for a while when—*Hmm?*

"…Loki?"

"Wha—?! S-Soma?!"

Without any warning, a god with black hair loomed over her. Soma sluggishly tilted his head as Loki was taken by surprise. Soma was the God of Sake. An eccentric even among the gods, he had descended to the mortal realm to brew all sorts of flavorful alcohol. His familia had gotten into the business, to the point where they had a brewery apart from their home. Loki liked to brag that she and alcohol went together like a hand in a glove, and he was an acquaintance who she had interacted with a couple of times because she wanted to drink some of his homemade sake.

"What are you doing here…?"

"That's my line!" she yelped.

He had long hair for a guy, and his bangs swept over his eyes, covering them. Saying he was gloominess incarnate would not be wrong. Loki often teased him, calling him a God of Hobbies because he was always holed up, immersed in making sake. To see an introverted god out and about was half the reason Loki was so surprised.

"My brewery is close to Daedalus Street…"

"Ah…that's right, you mentioned that before. Taking a shortcut?"

"Yeah…"

"But this area's off-limits. You know if you get caught, Ganesha will fly right off the handle."

"That's why I was doing it in a way that wouldn't stand out…"

She looked exasperated as Soma muttered in a subdued voice. The idea of him somehow being Enyo was just too ridiculous for her to seriously entertain.

However, he did seem to assume the role of a patron god more than when they'd first met. She did not know what caused this change of heart, but…Loki wasn't really in a place where she could care at the moment.

"I won't tell anyone. Hurry up and beat it." She shooed him away.

"I'll take my leave…"

Loki sighed as the god aimlessly started walking hunched over.

"—Divine Wine." As he was moving past, Soma suddenly halted, whipping around to look at her.

"Huh?"

"—I smell a gods' brew." Soma closed in, expressionless, his eyes opened wide behind his hair.

Taken aback by his sudden change in demeanor, Loki was overwhelmed.

"Loki, you had Divine Wine?"

"D-don't be stupid! I haven't even had one drop of your real stuff! You wouldn't ever share any with me! Even though I really wanted to try it! Actually, I could really, really, really use some right about now!" Loki pleaded her innocence with so much force that spittle started flying, but Soma was persistent.

"No. Not mine. It doesn't smell like what I make."

"Huh?"

"This is something made by someone else."

"I tell you not to be stupid, and you gimme that? Who other than you is making it in the mortal realm...?"

"But I definitely smell it on you."

Loki shrank back as he sniffed all around her with the fervor of a dog. She was still a goddess, after all, so if some stupid deity started getting cozy and smelling her, she would obviously want to drop an iron fist on the top of his head, but...she raised her arm to her nose to catch a whiff.

However, even Loki, who loved every kind of booze, could not detect the faintest scent of alcohol.

"It doesn't smell like you actually drank it yourself...I'm guessing it rubbed off from someone else..."

"From someone...else...?"

"Loki, you know a drinker?" Soma asked as he leaned in.

This was coming from a god who everyone struggled to hold a conversation with. He had a totally new sparkle in his eyes.

"Loki, I want to know. Who else is making divine alcohol down here?"

"W-wait! Wait! I'm telling you, I don't remember anything...!" Loki held both her arms out to keep him back as Soma cornered her, suddenly becoming a chatterbox.

"The process and the type of alcohol are different...Grapes...Is it a grape wine?"

When she heard those words, her heart started beating like crazy.

"…"

An electric spark. Her thoughts flickered. She realized her heart was pounding harder than normal. And with her throat quivering, she arrived at a single answer.

"It can't be…" Her eyes snapped open, and in the next moment, she started running. "Soma, come with me!"

As Loki launched off, Soma obediently tagged along.

Booking it out of Daedalus Street, they headed for the city's southeast corner to a place that she'd never been before, but she knew the location. For several reasons, including an abundance of caution, it was a home that she had never tried to approach previously.

Out of breath as she slammed into several people on the street, Loki finally arrived at that building.

"*Huff…Wheeze…!* Here…"

Dionysus Familia's home. As expected, there wasn't even a hint of a soul at the luxurious manor that no longer had anyone left to return to it.

If a familia was disbanded or destroyed because its patron god was sent back, its property and funds were reclaimed by the Guild, but that had not happened yet, since *Dionysus Familia* had been destroyed only hours ago. The Guild did not have the time to spare with all the things already stacked high on its plate. All the objects should still be there.

"This smell…Over here."

Before Loki could ask, Soma started moving around to the back side of the manor. She did not even have the time to tease him for acting like a pooch.

She just tailed after him and scrambled over the back fence. Normally, they would have already been caught by a familia member on guard and marched off the premises, but there was no one left anymore. After snooping in the backyard, they snuck into the manor, following Soma's nose—and found the stairway connecting to the underground room.

"This is…"

As they opened the door, unfolding before them were shelves lining the walls that held countless bottles. It was the wine cellar Dionysus had built.

In any other circumstance, Loki would have rejoiced at the untold number of famous labels in storage—a horde of treasure before her eyes. The cool air of the cellar caused them to shiver as they quickly stepped inside.

Finally, Soma stopped sniffing, standing in front of a shelf in one corner of the room. Following his gaze, Loki retrieved a single bottle from the shelf. Her fingers trembling, she popped open the cork. A bewitching sweet smell wafted from it.

"…There's no mistaking it. This is Divine Wine."

She gasped at his declaration as he continued to rave, unable to mask his shock and interest.

"This is…even more complete than mine."

Loki looked at him in wonder. That was impossible. Unbelievable. *Who the hell could have created something to make Soma say that…?*

He said one last thing, breaking through the unending stream of doubts and questions rushing through Loki's head.

"This…*would get even a god completely drunk.*"

"_____"

Those words and their meaning sent a flash of understanding through Loki's mind. Dionysus the manipulated. Dionysus the fool. Drunk. Drunk. Drunk. Had he been drunk? Had Dionysus been *drunk*? What if he had been made to habitually drink Divine Wine? What if he had been sipping on it every day without realizing it, getting smashed and manipulated like a puppet? What if he had been drunkenly guided to catch Loki's and Hermes's attention, toward maintaining a feud with Ouranos, whose side protected the order of the city?

This could do it… This wine could totally do that!

She was sure of it, peering at the alcohol in front of her that was even starting to mess with her senses from a single whiff. At the same time, the scent of grapes triggered something in her memories.

"...I *know* this. This smell. *I know this smell!*"

I've smelled this before somewhere else!

Gripping the bottle with both hands, she stared at it as if glaring into the eyes of her foe.

Where? Where did I smell it? Where the hell did I smell this before...?!

The mark on the label was one that even Loki did not recognize, resembling an emblem, a stemmed glass overflowing with wine.

A tavern? Impossible! They'd never have something like this! A brewery? No, I haven't been to one! Not the drink itself but the ingredients, maybe...Grapes...Grapes...Grapes?

As she looked at the bloodred wine rolling around inside the bottle, a hazy memory limply started to distort.

Dionysus had been drinking wine next to *a certain person*...

"*—I am very particular when it comes to grape wine—*"

Dionysus had walked up to Loki.

"*—and this is absolutely superb.*"

He had been standing next to...

"It can't be..." Her vermilion eyes snapped wide open.

"It can't be?!" she shouted, which came out like a pained scream.

"Ouranos."

In the Chamber of Prayers at Guild Headquarters, Fels's black robe billowed.

"The results?"

"I'll start with the conclusion: Knossos has transformed into a spirit realm."

While *Ganesha Familia* was observing it from aboveground on Daedalus Street, Fels had been investigating it with the Xenos from the eighteenth floor. The mage in black robes had returned to report back.

"I'm guessing it's a miracle triggered by spirits or something along those lines. It resembles what the Sword Princess and the others saw at the pantry on the twenty-fourth floor and what Lido and the Xenos dealt with on the thirtieth floor. But this is something else entirely. Or perhaps it would be better to say it is on an entirely higher level."

"..."

"The green flesh filling all the passages has agency and attempts to eliminate any intruders. It's the first time we've ever had to take on an actual dungeon i-itself," Fels announced, faltering slightly.

The mage felt incredibly reluctant to describe that hideous green flesh as the result of a spirit miracle.

"It is probably a parasitic reaction caused by the use of multiple demi-spirits…The method is unclear, but there's no doubt that it's related to the power of the corrupted spirit."

Knossos had been reborn as a castle for the devil. Fels's conclusion was that it had become an even more repulsive and stout fortress.

"If we were to burn and dig it all out…it would take a lot of time and effort. At the very least, it would take one or two days just to reach the floor where the spirits are hidden. It's best to consider it impossible to invade Knossos while it's in this state."

And that was fatal—with the countdown to Orario's destruction still moving forward. Fels's black gloves clenched, and then the mage breathed out and relaxed their grip.

The four torches set on the altar flickered as Ouranos spoke. "I'm guessing this was the aim from the beginning. If *Loki Familia* did not attempt to clear Knossos, then our foes would simply have bided their time until the destruction of the city. And if anyone did try to attack…they had the option to use the remnants of the Evils as a sacrifice and annihilate the invaders."

"Are you saying the Evils' Remnants were sacrificial pawns?"

"Tools with some utility, perhaps," Ouranos corrected, his blue eyes narrowing.

Fels's hooded head shook left and right limply.

"The devil's work…Are you saying that we were all just dancing around in the palm of Enyo's hand with the Evils and even *Loki Familia*?"

"No other conclusion is possible."

Fels's head swayed once again in awe of the enemy's cunning, by the figure of the god whose face none had yet seen.

"…I will continue the investigation on the progression of Knossos, but the problem is that we still don't know the identity of Enyo—or even have any suspects."

Ouranos shook his head.

"We have suspects," the god announced as he looked up at the ceiling shrouded in darkness. "Every single god and goddess in this city."

The city—no, the labyrinth that had been reborn as a demon's castle—sneered, burbling with a giggle, asking a single question.

"Enyo! Who are yooou?"

Something chirped in the darkness.

Far removed from the mortal realm, only the heavens above had all the answers.

Status
Lv.4

STRENGTH:	C 601	ENDURANCE:	C 602
DEXTERITY:	C 603	AGILITY:	C 604
MAGIC:	I 0	HUNTER:	H
IMMUNITY:	H	SPEED:	I

MAGIC: None

SKILLS: None

EQUIPMENT: Protagonista

- A standard single-handed sword.

- Made by *Hephaistos Familia*. Its cost is confidential.

- His cohort, Anakity, forced him to take this weapon—unable to look the other way
  when he was swindled and lost everything, including the familia's earnings from an
  expedition, after getting swindled by a certain prostitute.

- Very sturdy and exceptionally sharp. But that's all it really offers—with no special
  powers to speak of. However, Raul has lovingly used it ever since, and it shows no
  signs of breaking.

- Raul Nord is an ordinary person with no skills or magic. Despite having no special
  weapons, Anakity trusts her back to him more than anyone.

EQUIPMENT: Noble Bow

- A standard bow and arrows. Made of wood.

- A virtuous bow constructed by an elven craftsman. It had been presented to Riveria,
  who was at a loss for what to do with it and, at Finn's suggestion, gave it to Raul.

- One of the weapons wielded by Raul, who had been critically lacking in dexterity.
  In the past, he had gotten depressed when Bete said he was not living up to the
  weapon's name, but it frequently sees use when he is in the middle and back of
  formations.

- Despite having no special qualities, Raul is always striving to become a first-tier
  adventurer, and Finn has confidence in him.

RAUL NORD

Raul • Nord

BELONGS TO:	*Loki Familia*	**JOB:**	adventurer
RACE:	Human	**WEAPONS:**	sword, bow and arrow, spear, ax, hammer
DUNGEON RANGE:	fifty-ninth floor		
CURRENT WORTH:	16,888,000 valis (including savings)		

Afterword

This is the eleventh book of the side story, brought to you by an author who has missed yet another deadline.

Please allow me to extend my sincerest apologies to the editors at GA Bunko, Kiyotaka Haimura, and all those involved…!

I know I've been including more and more spoilers in the afterwords. Be warned! This is the case here, too.

I've written this book with a great deal of effort. Take this as both a conclusion to a long battle and a catalyst for something else.

I knew it would irk people on multiple fronts (particularly those involved with the manga, game, anime, etc.), but this was still where it ended up. I have a conclusion in mind, and while I can't say for sure whether it was the right choice, I've set my foot down on this one.

In this volume, we didn't get another one of those miracles like we got in the eighth volume of the side story. I might regret the fact that I didn't save it for this book. In fact, the person who wrote this volume might just be the most unsure of all, so let's switch topics.

I'm going to forcibly segue into a happy topic: I was finally able to portray a battle scene for the holy woman. The Saint has been appearing since the first volume of the side story (and the fourth volume of the main series), but she just never got a chance to join and fight together with the main team in this series…I think that might have been the most exhilarating scene in this overall distressing volume. Her character design is actually one of my favorites out of the ones that Kiyotaka Haimura created, and I had always wanted to let her get her hands dirty.

When I presented my first draft, I was happily talking off my editor's ear: "Actually, I was thinking Amid would have this kind of background!" or "If that happened, and then *this* happened, which means this couple might be a thing!" or "Basically, what I'm trying to say is that she's really strong! Super strong! Like, ultra-hyper-strong!"

And every time, my editor told me very politely: "Please write that in the *Chronicle* series. *Grin.*"

I can't promise that I'll absolutely write that in the next manuscript, because I obviously don't want to be *that* type of person. In fact, I'm not sure whether I'm expressing myself very well, but I bet the holy woman will play an active role from time to time. Make sure to keep an eye out for her in the future. Let's just say: Yes, I'm working on a bunch of manuscripts.

Moving along. Lately, as I'm writing, I find myself thinking that foreshadowing is difficult.

Like, even when I'm secure in my decision and the plot is moving forward, there have been times when I get an "oh shit" moment at my wits' end when I come back to it.

I guess there are a lot of factors to blame: my insufficient situational awareness, not adding enough details in earlier scenes, etc. At its core, the main reason is a lack of experience for me.

I mean, obviously, both the author and the readers open up a new book knowing nothing. Whether I can arrive at the scene in my head is sort of like a series of adventures. And in all those trips, there are only a handful of examples of foreshadowing that were set up and later ultimately paying off. Or at least, that's how it has been with my works so far.

Recently, I've started to get a feel for the rhythm of battles. Or at least I think I have. But weaving in foreshadowing and the cathartic payoff associated with it are still a bit of a mystery to me.

I wouldn't say that I'm scared to set up foreshadowing, but I would say that I've gotten to the point where it takes courage for me to weave it into the story. Perhaps I'm being too cautious, since I can always just abandon some of the earlier details, but I really want to be able to add more spice to the story. I want to be able to say: "It was planned all along!" and flash a smug grin, following in the footsteps of many people in the story.

And as always, I worry whether I did a good job following through on the foreshadowing this time, but I will continue to battle against this inner demon going forward.

With that, I'd like to move to my words of gratitude.

To my editor Takahashi and chief editor Kitamura, I'm in your debt once again. I'm sorry for always keeping the editorial department in a time crunch.

To Kiyotaka Haimura for the illustrations. I hope you will let me use a few of the wonderful character designs that I couldn't employ at some later time...!

My sincere apologies to everyone involved who helped this book make it to publication. And as always, thank you very much to all the readers who picked up this book.

My plan is to bring this long battle to its end in the next volume.

Speaking of, why did this big massacre have to happen on the heels of the events in the thirteenth volume of the main series? Why would you plot this scheme, Enyo? Give me a break! And all my other grievances should hopefully be cleared in the next book...

I hope I will be joined by the readers as I continue to believe in hope and run through to the end. I would love it if you would come along with me on this journey.

To everyone who read this far, thank you very much.

And with that, I'll take my leave.

Fujino Omori